THE PROMETHEUS CONSPIRACY

CARL RICHARDSON

Matador
9 Priory Business Park,
Wistow Road, Kibworth Beauchamp,
Leicestershire. LE8 0RX
Tel: 0116 279 2299
Email: books@troubador.co.uk
Web: www.troubador.co.uk/matador
Twitter: @matadorbooks

ISBN 978 1788030 007

British Library Cataloguing in Publication Data.
A catalogue record for this book is available from the British Library.

Printed and bound by CPI Group (UK) Ltd, Croydon, CR0 4YY
Typeset in 11pt Aldine401 BT by Troubador Publishing Ltd, Leicester, UK

Matador is an imprint of Troubador Publishing Ltd

MIX
Paper from
responsible sources
FSC
www.fsc.org   FSC® C013604

ABOUT THE AUTHOR

Born and brought up in West Cumbria, Carl Richardson studied at Manchester Polytechnic and Newcastle University. He spent most of his working life as a civil servant, having now retired.

1

The queue for the night shift at Sellafield's North Gate edged forward slowly as, one by one, cars at the head of the queue were waved through the gate by the police constable on guard. Every few seconds a pair of headlights swept past in the opposite direction, representing the advance echelons of the back shift who had managed to escape early. It was twenty minutes to midnight. Martin Little eased forward to keep up with the car in front, bringing the gatehouse into view, brightly lit, and with pole raised. A few minutes later he was through, and driving round to the B1600 complex along the perimeter road. Access to the B1600 complex was still through the old North Gate, even though it was part of the new build, which Martin Little found irritating. The new road would make his journey from Whitehaven a lot quicker, cutting out the queues at the North Gate; but everything south of the old Yottenfews Lane and west of the approach road to the old Main Gate was still in the hands of the construction companies, including the new road. They seemed to be taking an awfully long time to finish the job.

He parked and walked over to the gate. The B1600 complex was inside its own security fence, and he used his identity card to swipe himself through. The main building in the complex was B1602, which contained the Small Research Reactor, or SRR. Despite the reactor's name, B1602 was a big building, 40 feet high and 200 feet long, the biggest building in the complex. Another card swipe at the entrance required Martin's identity card again. Inside, he went to the changing rooms and changed into an anti-contamination suit, boots and hard hat, and attached a new film badge. Dave Turner came in while he was changing. Dave was shift manager on this shift roster.

"You're in early tonight."

"Aye, managed to get away a bit sooner. Carole was back early from work, so she fixed us some supper."

"Will you be at Penrith on Saturday?"

Egremont Rugby Club were playing away at Penrith. Martin and Carole now lived in Whitehaven, but Martin was originally from Egremont and was still an occasional supporter of the club.

"No, Carole wants us to go shopping in Newcastle Saturday. I've kept promising her we'll go, so we've fixed it up for this Saturday. Why, are they going to win for a change?"

"Well, there's always hope, or miracles."

"They're going to need a few miracles, the way they've been playing the last few games."

"Aye, likely."

Others were coming into the changing room as the rest of the shift arrived. Greetings were exchanged, and Martin and Dave made their way out and down to the main office. In the office, the shift manager and shift foreman of the back shift were waiting to do the handover. Les Docherty, the shift manager, went through the checklist with Dave Turner.

"The reactor is now completely shut down, and all controls are at nominal settings. All the remote handling equipment has been checked and is ready for unloading. We've cleared the bay, and all the bay equipment is ready. If you'd like to sign off…"

Dave did so.

"You've had a busy night then?"

"Aye, we've not had an unloading shift for a while. We had to draw the short straw eventually, I suppose."

"Where's His Nibs? Does he not do handovers?" This was a reference to the technical manager, Alan Southam.

"He's still down in the bay somewhere. He's doing the extra shift, so you'll be having the pleasure of his company."

"Blimey, what's got into him? Is he short of money, or what?"

"God knows. But you'll have plenty of time to ask him yourself."

Dave Turner followed Docherty and the others out of the office. In the main hall, members of both shifts assembled for the handover. Dave checked the shift roster to confirm that all of the night shift had arrived. With the handover completed, the back shift made their way towards the exit.

Down in the main equipment bay, Martin Little found that Alan Southam had been busy. He was assembling carrier frames for the irradiated sheets they were to unload. It seemed to Martin that there were more frames than they were going to need. Possibly the back shift hadn't assembled enough carrier frames. They were complex pieces of kit, combining a strong, lightweight lifting frame with radiation shielding incorporating lead sheeting. It didn't particularly matter if there were too many carrier frames – it was a normal practice in the nuclear industry to have more tools and equipment available than the minimum needed for the job in case a problem arose which suddenly required a replacement tool. If necessary they could leave the job of disassembling surplus carrier frames to the day shift. It was odd that Southam was doing the job himself, though. It was the sort of thing that would normally be done by the process workers on the shift.

Southam glanced at Martin as he approached.

"Busy?" Martin asked, opening the conversation.

"Aye. I didn't think there were enough carrier frames laid out by the back shift. They haven't done an unloading shift for a while, so possibly they weren't up to the unaccustomed workload."

Martin's sympathies were with the back shift, so he didn't respond to the jibe. Southam was from somewhere down country, as well as being middle class and university educated – an outsider. Ordinary Cumbrians like Martin didn't have anything to do with his sort; not outside work, at least.

"Is everything else ready?"

"Just about. All the unloading equipment's in place. The only thing that remains to be done is to unlock the radioactive store. I'll do that in a minute, after I've had a pee."

He finished assembling the last carrier frame, then made his way over to the men's toilets in the bay area of the building. Once inside, he took out his mobile phone, switched it on, and began to send a text message, while keeping an ear open in case anyone else came into the toilets. Mobile phones were not allowed inside B1602, which meant that, normally, people left them in their cars.

By 12.30 am, everything was ready for the unloading operation. The outer door of the airlock was opened after the air exchange process was completed. A remotely controlled electric trolley then pulled a train of four-wheeled flatbeds into the airlock, which was then closed. After a further air exchange, the inner airlock door was opened, and the trolley pulled the flatbeds into the reactor space. It was brought to a halt in front of an array of square sheets of metal held upright in metal stands. On each flatbed there was a carrier frame in the open position. The next operation, to lift the metal sheets out of their stands, place them into the carrier frames, and then close the frames, was carried out manually.

One of the process workers, Shona Graham, operated remote handling devices through the wall of the reactor space to lift the metal sheets, while looking through specially shielded windows. It was a job she had been trained to do, for which she received extra pay, as there were extra hazards involved in doing this job. With the sheets transferred, she then closed each of the carrier frames. The train of flatbeds was then removed from the reactor, going through the airlock procedure in reverse. Once out of the reactor, the trolley pulled the flatbeds, with their cargo, into the radioactive store, where each one was unloaded by two process workers. Although the metal sheets were radioactive, once enclosed in the lead shielding of the carrier frames, they were safe to handle for short periods.

Over the next hour, three more unloading operations were carried out in the same way, unloading a total of twelve of the metal sheets. With the unloading completed, there was the opportunity for a break, and all the members of the shift made their way to the rest room opposite the main equipment bay. There was a coffee machine and a vending machine for snacks, a kettle and a microwave oven. It was a bit primitive, but it was just about adequate. Less easy to get used to, for the smokers at least, was the fact that they couldn't even stand outside the door to the building and have a smoke. It was forbidden to bring smoking materials into the B1600 complex at all, which made the full eight-hour shift something of a trial for the heavier smokers. But there was always some banter to lighten the mood and keep things going.

"Are your lot of geriatrics really going all the way to Penrith Saturday?" someone called out to Martin.

Martin smiled. "Super geriatrics, maybe."

"Are you sure the bus ride won't tire them out? There'll need to be lots of toilet breaks on the way – with the first one at Bigrigg."

There was general laughter.

Someone else called out, "Speaking of toilets, where's His Nibs? He's always skulking in the bogs."

"I think he's trying to pick up a bloke for a shag."

"He always goes into the cubicles 'cause he sits down to piss like a woman."

"There's nowt wrong with being a woman," shouted out Shona Graham.

"Not with being a real woman, love; only a ponsie poof like that bastard Southam."

There was laughter and jeers, which were loud enough to obscure any noises from outside. However, Dave Turner, who happened to be right by the door to the room, did hear a noise above the shouting and laughter in the room – something between a bang and a thump, from somewhere in the bay or the main hall outside.

He opened the door and had a quick look out. There was nothing unusual that he could see. He stepped out, closing the door behind him. He walked along to the corner of the corridor and turned into the main hall. Almost immediately he was confronted by a number of men dressed entirely in black.

For a moment, he assumed they were site police – a special unit of constabulary for the Sellafield site – but a second look told him that they were something else. They were dressed in combat fatigues, which were all black rather than in disruptive camouflage. They wore military boots and steel helmets, also all black; and each carried a short-barrelled automatic weapon. His initial impression was that there were three of them; but he then saw that there were a lot more of them behind the leading three. All were dressed in the same black combat uniforms, and all were carrying automatic weapons. He wondered how they had got in: the main outside door was closed and looked intact. Any attempt at unauthorised entry there would have set off alarms.

Then he saw a hole about 3 feet across in the end wall near the door, and on the floor several feet away, a jagged piece of the wall that had been blown out. Dave Turner had never heard of detonating cord; but he was now looking at the results of its use. He stopped, unsure of what to do. The soldiers continued towards him, and moments later there were several machine gun barrels pointing at his stomach from a few feet away.

One of the soldiers spoke, in clear English, but with a pronounced foreign accent.

"Put your hands up, and turn to face the wall."

2

Alan Southam watched as the pebble he had thrown skipped across the still surface of the lake. Three, four, five, six times the smooth pebble bounced, creating an avenue of ripples on the placid water. Six times – was that lucky? He had left the flat in Whitehaven and driven out to Derwentwater to try and clear his head from the thoughts going round and round in his mind. Derwentwater was grey under a grey sky, with hardly any wind to disturb the water. The gravel of the shoreline crunched under his feet as he walked along the edge of the lake below Friar's Crag. Across the lake, the double humps of Cat Bells swept up towards Maiden Moor, dark against the sky. There was a sense of permanence about this place; a sense that, if one could stay there indefinitely, one's life might remain as unchanged as the lake and the hills.

But it was not so for him. His life had already changed substantially in the last year, and in every respect for the worse. His marriage of fourteen years to Hazel had ended in divorce. It had been an acrimonious divorce, and Hazel had taken him for everything he had. She had managed to persuade the court to deny him any access to their daughter Rachael, as well as being awarded the house in Gosforth which had been their home for nine of Rachael's twelve years. At a recent meeting, his solicitor had advised him that he had information that Hazel was preparing further claims against him, relating to his savings and pension.

"I've had a letter from her solicitor asking for further information about your pension, in view of reports of proposed pension enhancements for staff at Sellafield," his solicitor, Robin Jones, had told him. "I wanted to speak with you before making any response. Strictly speaking, you don't have to respond to such a query, as no changes have taken place yet, and in any event, your pension only reaches its final form once you begin to draw it. Basically, they're just fishing for information; but it's an indication of hostile intent, as it were."

"I hardly need reminding of that. The hostility of the court seems to be directed entirely towards me. I had thought that divorce was supposed to be 'no fault' these days; but I seem to have been targeted simply because I was the male partner in the marriage."

"Few in the legal profession would dispute that there's a serious problem in the law relating to divorce; at least not in private. In the short term, there's not much that anyone can do about it, other than get the best legal advice and assistance possible."

Southam doubted that many lawyers would be pushing for any changes in the divorce laws any time soon.

"But to make further claims, they would have to go back to the court."

"Yes, that's right; and at the moment, in my view, that isn't likely in the short term unless, for example, your circumstances were to change."

"For better or for worse?"

Robin Jones gave a humourless smile. "Obviously, they would only really be interested in the former; but changes either way could affect the situation. The only other factor that might change things is if new information became available about your existing situation. Hence this attempt to fish for more information, presumably."

"But if my situation were to change, I could go back to the court to ask for a change in the penalties imposed on me."

"Yes. In fact, you're required to notify the court of changes relevant to the divorce settlement. But of course, it will be the same court as before, with the problems you have just described. In any event, I would of course do my best to present your case."

Would he? Where was the advantage in defending a losing proposition, especially a losing financial proposition? As he had pointed out, it would be the same court, with the same laws and the same prejudices. For Robin Jones, it was just another case.

But now all that had been eclipsed. On Friday he had been called into the office of Hank Williamson, manager of the B1600 complex. The operation of the complex had been contracted out to Vermont Technical Services, a US management company. All the staff at the complex worked for VTS on short-term contracts, renewable six-monthly. It meant that all the staff, including qualified technical and scientific staff, were effectively casual labour with no employment rights, as the contracts also specified that they were classed as self-employed. Only senior managers and certain other favoured individuals had open-ended contracts with more secure employment. Needless to say, Hank Williamson was one of these.

"Bad news, I'm afraid. We won't be renewing your contract when it expires at the end of June."

Alan Southam had stared at him with a horrible feeling in the pit of his stomach. He had worked at Sellafield for nearly twenty years, and during that time had seen the conditions of employment steadily deteriorate as successive privatisations fragmented the organisation into a mess of competing operating companies, each interested only in the bottom line, and doing as little as possible to meet the terms of their contracts. The staff were always among the first casualties of this. He had witnessed each deterioration with dismay and apprehension lest it should signal his own redundancy. That event had now come to pass.

"Will I be offered redeployment?"

"No redeployment is taking place, as all the operating companies are downsizing."

"That means I would have to leave the site; leave the area. There's no alternative employment in this area for someone with my skills and qualifications."

"I'm afraid that will be your problem. The downsizing is intended to reduce the number of personnel on the payroll. You have my sympathy, as there will be a lot of people in your position; but unfortunately these decisions have to be implemented."

"You'll be short of cover on the Technical Section. You'll be in danger of violating the risk assessment parameters."

"We've gone into that, and we think we'll be able to manage. It'll require extra commitment from the remaining staff, but I'm sure they will understand the situation."

"Why me? Why was I chosen for redundancy?"

"It wasn't an easy decision, but in the end it was felt that the other staff in the Technical Section had more to offer in terms of experience and expertise."

"I see."

He did see. He had an honours degree in physics from Birmingham University and was a member of the Institute of Electrical Engineers. Other members of the Technical Section had no such qualifications, having worked their way up through the ranks and gained promotion through personal influence. Personal influence was clearly at work here. He was being got rid of because his face didn't fit.

He had then abruptly turned and left the room. There was nothing more to be said. He was a nuclear engineer and had spent most of his working life at Sellafield because that was the place where his skills and expertise were best used and most needed. Now he was being discarded in favour of lesser-qualified timeservers who were always in favour because they were "our lads".

During the next few days, he started to absorb the shock of what had happened. Within the space of a year his life had fallen apart. He had lost his marriage and his family, and now his career. His work at Sellafield had not been just a job. It was what he had studied physics for all those years ago. Some of the work they had been doing recently with the Small Research Reactor was the kind of thing he had hoped one day to be involved in when, as a student, he had thought about his future. Nuclear physics had advanced a great deal during the course of his career, and he was fortunate enough to have been involved in some of that.

However, for some time now he had become increasingly

conscious of the change in the nature of the organisations that ran the nuclear industry. In the early days in the 1950s and 1960s, atomic energy and atomic power were the sole prerogative of the state, in the form of the UKAEA; and that was accepted without question because of the importance and even the mystique of all things "atomic". Since the 1970s, a succession of right-wing governments had fragmented and privatised the industry, degrading it in importance, until it had become what it was now: a mess of private operating companies, interested only in next quarter's balance sheet, squabbling over the corpse of a once great industry. Looking at this now, knowing he would shortly be leaving the industry, he suddenly saw it in much sharper focus. Perhaps… perhaps it wasn't such a bad thing to be leaving now, when all that the industry faced was further decline. But what would he do? Where would he go?

Enquiries he made during that week confirmed the bleakness of his situation. All the organisations in the nuclear industry he contacted told him the same story: they were either downsizing and shedding staff, including technical and scientific staff, or at least, not taking on any extra staff in the near future. Employment agencies he contacted told him the same story. The only overseas jobs the agencies had on their books were in France, where the large French nuclear industry continued to be supported by the French Government. However, all these jobs required applicants to be fluent in the French language. The nuclear industry was undergoing a unique decline, due not only to the global trade recession, but also to the aftermath of the Fukushima nuclear disaster in Japan, and the resultant political unpopularity of nuclear power.

As he took in the situation, it looked increasingly obvious that his career was at an end. His next job, assuming he was lucky enough to find one, would be just that: a job. He might even have to accept a menial job of some kind if that was all he could find. His career as a nuclear engineer was over, and at the age of 44 he was too old to start a new career. In more normal times, if he had been unable to find another job in the nuclear industry in Britain, he would have been prepared to move to the US or Canada, or even Australia, to progress his career. That would have been a particularly attractive option now, given the unpleasant consequences of his divorce. But all those options were now closed.

Something within him baulked at the idea of accepting this defeat. It was more than just a matter of pride. A professional career becomes part of the identity of the person following it, part of how he defines himself as an individual. It cannot simply be discarded like a suit of old clothes. He was a nuclear engineer, and that would define his future as well as his past. There had to be something for him. Which organisation, anywhere in the world, would still welcome his services as a nuclear engineer, with the particular knowledge and experience that he had?

The answer came to him immediately, as if it had been waiting in his subconscious for him to ask the question in that form. For several minutes he sat very still, turning the idea over in his mind. There was no doubt that they would want what he had to offer, but... it might be dangerous – bloody dangerous. What else? Loyalty? To whom? To what? For what purpose? And the consequences? Once he committed himself, there would be no going back. Would it be possible to find out what they might offer him without committing himself?

At length, he needed a respite from the thoughts chasing round in his head. He left the flat, got into his car, and drove out to Derwentwater, his favourite place in the Lake District. Standing looking at the wide vistas across the still waters of the lake, he began to think more clearly.

3

The journey down to London had been uneventful but tiring, as Southam had not staged the journey, stopping only once at a service station on the M6. Consequently, he wasn't able to do anything more on that first evening than go for an evening meal at the hotel's restaurant, have a bath and retire to bed. The following day he went out shortly after breakfast, browsed around the shops in the vicinity of the hotel for a couple of hours, then returned to his hotel room, having thus allowed time for the room to be serviced. He could then remain in the room undisturbed for the rest of the day. It was inevitable that he would be caught on some street surveillance cameras, but he would do what he could to minimise his exposure to them. He slept for a while, and then between 6 and 7 pm he had some coffee and ate a sandwich and some biscuits he had bought that morning.

Shortly afterwards he left the hotel. He got into his car, a Toyota estate, and drove the few hundred yards to another hotel, which he had selected after some study of it on the internet. He turned into the entrance and parked at the far end of the hotel car park. This was a risky part of his plan, but necessary if it was to work. He was gambling that no one at the hotel would realise in the next few hours that this car did not belong to a hotel resident. He opened the boot and took out false number plates, which he fitted over the existing ones. He then left the hotel car park and made his way on foot towards Soho Square.

On reaching the square, he walked round it, investigating each of the streets running off it in turn. From these he could look down the smaller side streets, and at length he found what he was looking for. On two or three of the smaller streets there were women standing at intervals along the pavement. He had to make an assessment of what he saw as he walked past the entrance to each street without stopping. Having looked down each street in this way, he returned to one of them and started to make his way down the street. As he passed them the women smiled at him, and some called out to him.

"Are you looking for pleasure, sir? Would you like some pleasure tonight?"

He smiled back without speaking and walked on. At the end of the street he turned and walked back up the street again, stopping in front of the woman who had caught his eye on the way down. Of all the women on that street, she was the nearest in appearance to what he had in mind. She was much older than all the others, some of whom were little more than children – she was perhaps in her late forties or early fifties. She looked Southern European. For a moment, they looked at each other, she smiling. He smiled back.

"Do you have anywhere to go?" he asked.

Her smile was replaced by a worried look. "No. Do you?"

He smiled again. "Yes, but we'll have to walk."

She nodded, and they left the street together, followed by the curious stares of some of the other women.

"Where are you from?" he asked her after they had been walking for a couple of minutes.

"I am from Greece. I'm a teacher of modern languages. I came to England to find work, because there is nothing in Greece. There is no hope in Greece now. The politicians have destroyed the public services to pay off the debts of their business friends, so my only hope of finding work was to go to another country. In England I could work as a teacher and send money to my family in Greece. But now the same thing is happening here. I was made redundant last year and cannot find another job as a teacher. My family in Greece are dependent on me sending money to them. And so, when I need money to send to my family, I have to do this."

He reflected that in different ways they were both in the same situation: having been rejected in their professions, they were having to sell what they could in order to survive.

They reached the hotel where he had parked his car. It was still there, evidently still undetected. They got into the back of the car. He had put blinds up against all the rear windows, and he now rigged a curtain across the car just behind the front seats. He lowered the back seats, and laid out a couple of camping mattresses to form a bed.

He asked her what she charged. It was a bit more than he had expected when he had set out that evening, but it made his main task easier. They undressed sitting on the back seat. She was a mature woman: her breasts were heavy and pendulous, but very full; her broad hips gave her a gorgeously broad belly. He drew her to him and kissed her, luxuriating in her softness.

"It would help if you could let me enjoy your bottom first."

She turned and lay full length on her tummy, presenting her bottom to him. Her broad hips gave her a big bottom, smooth and creamy white. His face sank into the sweet softness, and for the next few minutes he was in paradise.

Afterwards, as they lay together, he continued to hold her in his arms as his breathing slowly returned to normal.

He kissed her cheek gently. "Thank you," he said.

She nodded and smiled, then sat up to indicate that the session was over. He also sat up, and then stuck his head through the curtain and leaned into the front of the car, retrieving a large envelope from its hiding place. She had started to dress, putting her bra and pants back on. He opened the envelope and took out the amount of money she had asked for, but letting her see that there was a lot more money in the envelope. He gave her the money he had taken out.

"If you will do one more thing for me tonight, I will give you a thousand pounds."

He opened the envelope so she could see the wad of banknotes that filled it.

"One thing? What do you mean?" She wondered what kind of sex he wanted that he would offer so much money for it. It was a fear that she had to live with.

"I want you to deliver a letter for me."

"A thousand pounds, just to deliver a letter?"

"I can't really explain in detail. But I can't be seen delivering the letter myself. I need someone to deliver it for me. You might get some idea when you see the place."

"Where is it, this place?

"Here in London, a few minutes' drive away. I will drive us to within sight of the building. I will then give you two hundred pounds. For the other eight hundred, you must walk over to the front door of the building, ring the bell, hand the letter in to the person who opens the door, then walk back to the car."

"Is this something illegal?"

"No." Since she had no idea what was in the letter, or what it was about, she was not in any way culpable. For him, it would be different; but she didn't need to know that.

She knew it must be something dodgy, but... a thousand pounds. It would mean she wouldn't have to do this for another month at least, maybe more. She was silent for another minute before she spoke.

"Alright."

He nodded. They both finished dressing and then got into the front seats of the car. A minute later they were driving west towards Kensington. On Kensington Road, while they were stopped at traffic lights, he produced a face mask from the door pocket and put it on. It was just a piece of plain brown card with eye-holes and a nose flap.

"It's just in case there are cameras," he said, to reassure her. She had looked alarmed when she saw him put it on.

A minute later, they had arrived. He pulled in at the entrance to a length of imposing terraced houses, four storeys high, on Prince of Wales Terrace. The entrance gave onto a length of road running in front of the terrace, off Kensington High Street but separated from it by a low wall. It was a wide entrance, so he was not blocking it. His luck was still holding. The security guard who patrolled that section of terrace was half way along it, walking away from them.

"Right, this is it. Two hundred pounds." He handed her the money, which she stuffed into a pocket, the tension clearly telling on her.

"This is the letter." It was a small envelope, very thin – there was only a single piece of paper in it – enclosed in clear cellophane, which had previously been the wrapper for a greetings card. There was something scrawled on the front of the envelope in a non-European script.

"Now, here's what you do. It's the fifth door along – that one there. Go up to the door and ring the bell – it's on the left-hand side of the door. It should be answered within a minute."

He had tried phoning a few days earlier at about the same time in the evening to confirm that there would be someone in. It was a call from a payphone, and he had hung up without speaking when the phone was answered.

"When the door is opened, don't speak, but hold up this piece of paper for them to read."

She took it and looked at it. On the upper part of the paper was typed a message: "My name is Poppy. I cannot speak. I have been asked to deliver this letter. I do not know what is in the letter." On the lower part of the paper there was what appeared to be more of the same strange script that was on the front of the letter envelope.

"I presume your real name isn't Poppy. Don't tell me what your name is – it's best if I don't know. Hang on to this piece of paper – don't let them take it. When they've read it, take the letter out of the cellophane, and hand it to them. Are you clear about everything? Hold up the paper, but hang onto it. Take the letter out of the cellophane and hand it over. Then walk back here. OK?"

"OK."

"Right, go!"

She got out, feeling tense with nerves. The mask he was wearing intensified the sense of alarm she felt. Quickly she walked over to the building. To her dismay she saw that the security guard had reached the end of his beat and was now walking back towards her. She reached the door and rang the bell. The security guard, on seeing this, quickened his pace towards her. She did not know what she would do when he reached her. But the door opened first. A young man dressed in a well-pressed suit stood looking at her.

"Yes, can I help?"

She held up the paper, and he leaned forward to read it. He then looked up at her as she pulled the letter out of the cellophane and handed it to him. At that moment, the security guard came up.

"Hey, what's your business here, miss? Who are you and what do you want here?"

She looked at him, fear rising within her, but she didn't speak. She looked back at the young man. He was looking intently at what was written on the front of the envelope. He then looked up, first at the security guard. He held his hand up.

"It's alright," he said to the guard. "One moment please," he said to her. He pulled a phone out of his pocket, pressed a key and held the phone to his ear. After a few moments he started speaking in what she presumed was his native language. He finished speaking and looked at her again.

"If you can wait a moment please," he said.

To her it seemed like an eternity, with the security guard standing right next to her, and not knowing what he would do when she tried to leave.

After a minute or so another man appeared from behind the young man. He was older, perhaps in his thirties, but casually dressed. There was a brief conversation between the two. The young man showed the other the letter.

The older man took the letter and opened it. In the glimpse that she had of it, she saw more of the strange script. The older man read through it, staring at it intently. For a moment he continued to stare, and the rest of them stood in a strange tableau, waiting for his response. He looked up, first at her, then at the guard, and then, noticing it for the first time, at the car in the entrance to the terrace. But the car driver, in the right hand seat, could not clearly be seen. He looked back at the letter. Still looking at the letter, he said something to the younger man in their language. He then looked at the guard.

"There is no problem here. We are happy to accept this letter. The woman can go in peace. There is no need to detain her."

He looked at her and said: "Thank you."

She nodded, and immediately turned and started walking away towards the car. The guard, momentarily uncertain of what to do, set off after her a few seconds later. She quickened her pace, and the guard, fumbling with his mobile phone, didn't catch up with her before she reached the car. The guard started taking pictures with his phone from a few feet away as she was getting into the car. The car started moving even before the door was closed, leaving the guard taking pictures of it as it disappeared into the distance.

Inside the car, after fastening her seatbelt, the woman lay back in her seat, trembling with nervous reaction. After a minute she looked at the man, still a stranger to her, who was driving the car.

"I feel I have earned that thousand pounds. I felt for a minute that my life was in danger from the guard."

"Indeed you have," he said. "I'm going to drop you here."

He now needed to take the false number plates off the car as soon as possible, and he needed to drop the woman off before he could do that. He had turned left into Abingdon Road, and after 100 yards or so he pulled in to the kerb. He reached for the envelope containing the rest of the money and thrust it into her hands.

"The bit of paper you held up, and the cellophane: let me have them."

She passed them to him.

"Right, out you get, quickly."

She fumbled with the seatbelt and then the car door, and moments later she was standing on the pavement. She slammed the door shut, and watched as the car drove off down the street, its red tail lights diminishing in the gloomy light of the street lamps. Then it was gone.

It was an unceremonious end to an extraordinary incident. He had not said goodbye or thank you – probably he was under a lot of strain as well. Less than two and a half hours had passed since he had picked her up on the back street in Soho. It was unlikely that she would ever see him again; but she would be left with the memory of this night for a long time to come. But she was also left with the money. She opened the envelope in her hand. It was still full of banknotes – too many to count here, so she stuffed it under her top and held it in place with her arm. She wasn't sure exactly where she was, so she started to walk back up to Kensington High Street. She crossed the road, and on reaching Kensington High Street, turned left, and a minute later, hailed a taxi. As she did so, a police car passed her going the other way, siren sounding and blue lights flashing.

After dropping the woman off, Southam turned left at the end of Abingdon Road, onto Stratford Road. After a short distance he turned off Stratford Road into a narrow, dimly lit alley, and after 100 yards or so, at the darkest point between two of the widely spaced and not very effective street lamps, he pulled in to the side. He switched the car lights off, and got out of the car. He removed the false number plates and put them together into the boot, under the carpet that covered the boot floor. Back in the car, he pulled out from the side and drove slowly down the length of the alley, with the car lights still switched off. At the end he turned right, switching the car lights on as he did so. He then turned left, and a minute later he was on Cromwell Road travelling east.

Ten minutes later he was back at his hotel. As luck would have it, he was just in time for last orders in the hotel restaurant, so he had a late dinner before retiring to his room. He was in a state of elation. His meticulous planning had paid off: everything had gone like clockwork.

As far as he could tell, he had successfully breached the security barrier which monitored all communications between citizens and foreign governments.

It would take the police a little while to realise that – not until they had established the fact that the car registration the security guard had taken was indeed a genuine registration number of a similarly coloured Toyota estate, but one in another part of the country, which had presumably not been in London on that day. A liberal application of road dirt around the lower part of his car had made his own number plates effectively unreadable, preventing motorway cameras from recording his journey to London. His itinerary, both going and returning, took him off the motorway well clear of Cumbria, with the journey being completed via scenic routes without cameras.

The police would have to go to fairly extraordinary lengths, even to checking the owners of every Toyota estate in the country, before their trawl would be wide enough to reach him. Would such a trawl be justified, if they had no idea what was in the letter? Only the fact of where the letter had been delivered could justify it. But before there was any chance of the police reaching him, he was expecting to be contacted by his respondents, in whose hands his fate now lay.

4

A week later, Alan Southam was standing looking out over the wide expanse of another lake, this time more purposefully. The surface of Windermere had been ruffled into brisk wavelets by a stiff southerly breeze under a cool grey sky. Standing on the main jetty at Waterhead, he had a view right down the lake. It was still early in the season, and no pleasure craft moved on its surface. Nearby, expensive yachts rode at their moorings in the bay, still under winter covers, the clinking of many metal halyards against aluminium masts filling the air with a gentle musical tinkling. A mile down the lake, the tall white superstructure of one of the lake steamers stood out above the grey water as it made its stately approach to Waterhead. Alan Southam stood watching until the ship was a couple of hundred yards from the jetty, when he turned and walked back to where he had left his car in the Waterhead car park. He got into the car and then sat back and waited.

A few minutes later he saw in the wing mirror a man approaching the car. The man paused for a moment looking at the car, and then moved forward, opened the front passenger door, climbed in and closed the door.

"Are you Prometheus?" he asked. It was the identity

that Alan Southam had given himself for this meeting. Southam nodded.

"And the code word?" Southam asked. This had been on the piece of paper the woman had held up on the steps of the embassy when she delivered the letter, and had not been referred to again.

"Asia," replied the other. Southam nodded.

"I am Mercury," the man said, maintaining the thread. "You have some information for us?"

"Are you qualified to speak about the particular area of technical expertise involved?"

"I am. Certainly sufficiently to be able to evaluate your information. Do I take it that you don't speak our language?"

"I don't, no. I used online machine translations on my computer to produce the messages I used."

Mercury nodded.

"We thought so," he said. "You seem to have taken commendable security precautions in contacting us."

"For me, this is a serious business, so I've done everything possible to ensure that it will be successful. If it nevertheless fails – in other words, if the British authorities find out and intervene – it won't be for want of trying on my part. I've done the best I can, given that I've never been involved in this kind of thing before."

"Perhaps a real spy would never have dared to do anything so bold."

"Don't misunderstand me – I'm aware of the possible risks. If the police are sufficiently determined, they will eventually find me; but it will involve a long and laborious search, which will take time. My plan is to complete this business before they have time to find me."

"And after that, what then? What if they do find you?"

Southam shook his head. "You're jumping too far ahead. I can explain about that later; or rather, it will become evident. First of all, I need to establish that you understand the technical details of what this is about, and also the possible implications of it. Can you start by telling me what you know about technetium-99."

"Technetium is one of the rare metals, forty-third in the table of elements, and it belongs to the same group in the table as molybdenum. As a natural element it's extremely rare, occurring in no more than trace amounts in a few locations on the earth's surface. This means that even the smallest usable quantities of technetium have to be manufactured artificially. This can only be done in a nuclear reactor. The process is to irradiate targets of highly enriched uranium through a filter designed for this purpose. One of the products of this is molybdenum-99, which is then extracted from the target material in the next stage of the process. This isotope of molybdenum is very unstable, and rapidly transmutes into technetium-99 in a matter of weeks. There are a number of medical and industrial processes that use technetium-99, but the most significant use is in nuclear weapon design.

"Particular combinations of technetium-99 and other materials used as a tamper or neutron reflector in certain designs of implosion-type fission weapons are the most effective in terms of reducing the amount of fissile material needed in the core. The other components of the tamper are relatively easy to acquire, but production of the technetium is entirely dependent on the availability of highly enriched uranium. Where this is in short supply, then there is obviously a direct opportunity cost of using it for the production of technetium-99. At the moment, the people I represent would not be interested in producing technetium-99 from whatever limited quantities of highly enriched uranium that they might possess."

"Because they are still in the position that the opportunity cost of doing so would be too great."

"Exactly so."

This was the crux of the matter, and Southam knew that Mercury would be as misleading as possible about the true situation with regard to the availability of highly enriched uranium. But they had taken the bait. Mercury wouldn't be there otherwise.

"Presumably, though, they would regard a supply of technetium-99 from an outside source in a different light."

Mercury nodded slowly. "Doubtless they would. But as you will be aware, there are no outside sources capable of producing such material that would be willing to supply it."

"No. But there might nevertheless be another way of obtaining it."

"And that is what this meeting is about."

Southam nodded. "I'm a nuclear engineer, and I work at a facility at which technetium-99 is being produced in the way that you've just described. It's located on the Sellafield site, which is not far from here. Your people may well be aware of this facility already; and they may also be of the view that this is of no particular interest to them, as anything inside a fenced and guarded site in a NATO country is obviously out of reach. But that's only how it looks when seen from the outside. If there was both information and assistance from someone on the inside, then the situation would be very different."

Mercury was reflective for a moment. "Before you say any more about that, I must ask you to go into detail about the processes you use to create the molybdenum-99, including specifications and settings."

Southam had been expecting the question. It would help to authenticate Mercury as well as himself. He went through the procedures in detail, noting from Mercury's reactions that he understood and followed the technical detail in the narrative.

After asking a couple of questions about technical details, Mercury nodded and said, "It's clear enough that you know what you're talking about. However, it's still not clear how this might help us in any way. As you said just now, the people I represent may well be aware of the existence of this facility and the processes that are carried out there. But as you also said, it's a fenced and guarded site, so it's not clear what the particular interest might be."

"You need to look at the detail in order to see the opportunity, and it's the kind of detail that's only really available from insiders. Yes, there are fences, and yes, there are guards. The guards are located in guardhouses at the main gates or entrances to the Sellafield site. There are too few of them to patrol the whole site effectively, especially during the night, when they are down to essential manning. The chance of the B1600 complex seeing a guard or any of the site police during the night is low; and the chance of that happening in any randomly selected hour during the night is even lower. Some of the police have access to small arms, mostly hand guns; but the civilian guards are all unarmed. The fence is crossed by a bridge which carries waste discharge pipes across the railway, across the river, and down to a long spit of land which forms the coast at that point, and then into the sea. The bridge has razor wire security fences at either end, but as it's unguarded, that shouldn't be a problem for determined men with proper cutting equipment. Fences can be cut, and locked buildings broken into with the right equipment.

"But the key to all this is the information that on certain nights, at certain times, the irradiated sheets of enriched uranium will be out of the reactor, in their carrier frames, and the radioactive store, where they're kept until they're shipped out, will be unlocked and open. When they're shipped out it's always under armed guard; but the weak spot is when the sheets are taken out of the reactor, and the radioactive store is unlocked and open. At that point, there are only a few unarmed civilian workers around. The nearest police or guards are several hundred metres away, and most of them are unarmed."

Southam produced a folded piece of paper and opened it out. It was an enlargement of part of an Ordnance Survey map, showing the part of the Cumbrian coast that included the Sellafield site.

"This map illustrates my proposition. This is the B1600 complex, which is part of the new build to the north-west of the original Sellafield site. This building here is B1602, which contains the Small Research Reactor and the radioactive store. Just to the south of the B1600 complex, about two hundred metres, is the conduit that carries the waste discharge pipes. From the point where it passes through the main site boundary, here, a bridge carries it across the railway and the river to this spit of land, which separates the river from the sea and forms the coast at this point. The conduit reaches ground level and then disappears underground just as it reaches the foreshore on the seaward side of the spit. The place where it reaches the ground is surrounded by a security fence which forms a small compound around that point. The compound is not manned, and the fence is standard security fencing which is not alarmed. Where the conduit passes under this road, there's an access passage that runs through alongside the pipes. As you can see, I've drawn in all the security fences and gates in blue ink. Points where there are alarms or electronic security, including CCTV, are indicated with red ink.

"Now, if your people could land something like an elite commando unit in, say, platoon strength, on the beach at this point, at the compound around the place where the waste discharge pipes reach ground level, they could use the bridge to gain access to the main site, and reach building B1602 within a few minutes of first landing, with a good chance of reaching it without being detected. On the basis of information which I would supply, they would arrive at exactly the moment when all the irradiated sheets had been removed from the reactor, but the radioactive store was unlocked and open. The civilian staff in B1602 could be held up at gunpoint while the sheets were secured and removed. The raiding party could be back on the beach in under an hour, possibly still without an alarm being raised.

"Mobile phones aren't allowed in the B1600 complex, meaning it would be difficult for the alarm to be raised by anyone in the building during the raid, if you were able to cut the landline phone link, which I've indicated. Even if an alarm was raised, the landing place on the spit is difficult to access from the mainland other than across the bridge. The spit extends some distance up the coast before the river turns inland. In a number of ways, the geography of the place is ideally suited to a raid of this kind.

"That's my proposition. I don't know how you would organise a raid like that, but I've outlined the opportunity that can be created with inside information and help. Obviously it's up to the people you represent to decide how much they want the object of the raid: the irradiated sheets, and also the replacement sheets of enriched uranium, in their carrier frames, which will also be in the radioactive store at that moment."

Mercury was reflective for a moment. "It's certainly a very interesting proposition. As you say, it's up to the people I represent to decide how much they want these irradiated sheets. I don't know how they would go about launching such a raid. The immediate vicinity of the site might be poorly defended; but I imagine the main problem would be getting a raiding party to that location through the wider defence and security networks, and even more, getting them out again, especially once the alarm had been raised.

"There would also be intelligence security considerations, and obviously, some of those would relate to you. What's your motive for doing this, and what do you hope to get out of it?"

Southam gave an account of the main events of his life during the previous year. He spoke frankly, leaving nothing out, about the impending termination of his employment, and his views about the deteriorating situation at Sellafield and in the wider nuclear industry. He also spoke about his divorce, and the increasingly bitter situation with his former wife.

"It shouldn't be too difficult for your people to verify this information if they're looking for a motive. But don't misunderstand me about this either. It may look as if I'm doing this as an act of revenge against my employer, for making me redundant; or against the British Government. That isn't the case. This is purely about self-interest, not revenge. The problem for the British authorities is their assumption that loyalty is a one-way street: that no matter how badly they may treat an individual, that individual always owes a duty of loyalty to the Government and the state. The reality is that loyalty is symmetrical: if the state and its agencies show no loyalty to an individual and treat him badly, then they have no grounds to expect any loyalty from that individual. In my case, having been dumped by my employer, I need to move on and find a new opportunity, and one which enables me to continue in my chosen career as a nuclear engineer. If that happens to be with people the British authorities regard as hostile enemies, that's entirely their problem, not mine.

"That also answers your second question: what do I hope to get out of this? What I want is to come and work for your civil nuclear industry as a nuclear engineer. I can help your people set up the irradiation process for producing more molybdenum-99. But I also have more than twenty years' experience in the British civil nuclear industry, and I have a lot of expertise and information about processes that they use. So, if this expedition comes off, when the raiding party departs with the irradiated sheets, I want them to take me with them."

"That might be a big ask, nevertheless. There would obviously be a suspicion that you were a spy, planted by the British authorities in our nuclear industry."

"That's understandable. But acquisition of these irradiated sheets should enable your people to develop nuclear warheads very quickly – and not just nuclear warheads, but warheads miniaturised sufficiently to be fitted to ballistic missiles. I think that that would be regarded by both the British and American authorities as far too high a price to pay just to get a spy planted in your civil nuclear industry. I should stress that it's your civil nuclear industry I'm interested in, not your military programme. I don't have any expertise in nuclear weapons design, and I wouldn't expect to be given access to any of your military programmes.

"But that's the bottom line: if your people want these sheets, then what I want in return is a job as a nuclear engineer. I can supply the information about when the right moment will be, but if your people want these things, they will have to come and get them. And they don't have long – my contract terminates at the end of June."

5

The car wound its way along the dirt track, climbing all the while as the track followed a series of switchback bends in ascending the hill. As the track wound on, it climbed into a plantation of olive trees, the trees planted in neat lines which followed the contours of the hill. Although it was still only early in the day, even at this height the sun was already hot. But up here, at least the air was clear of the smog from the city which sprawled across the plain below, glimpsed occasionally through the trees. For Abdul Saeed, it was a welcome opportunity to escape, if only briefly, from the city; from its dusty heat, and from its ever watchful eyes.

At length, on a long straight stretch of track, a man appeared on the road from behind a line of olive trees about 100 metres ahead of the car. Saeed slowed, making ready to take evasive action. When he recognised the man, however, he brought the car to a stop beside him. Musa Khalid was his contact in the Defence Ministry. Khalid turned and indicated the space between the lines of trees behind him, where another car was parked. Saeed turned his car and parked alongside the other car, got out and closed the car door before turning to greet Khalid. As he did so, a third man emerged from the trees. Khalid introduced him.

"This is Hamid Rahman. He's from the military programme, although I can't say much more than that at present. However, it was because he was able to spare time today that this meeting became possible."

Saeed and Rahman shook hands.

They walked along the dusty avenue between two lines of trees until they reached a grassy space where they could sit down.

Saeed spoke first. "Right. First of all, the checks we have done on this character have all come back negative. In other words, his story has been substantially corroborated from independent sources. His name is Alan Southam. He's one of the project engineers on Project Mayfly at the Small Research Reactor at Sellafield. Project Mayfly is a project for carrying out what we call mediated transmutation, which involves irradiating targets of enriched uranium in such a way as to produce molybdenum-99.

"A major redundancy programme is being carried out at Sellafield in the near future, and while we cannot confirm independently that Alan Southam is being made redundant, all the circumstantial evidence corroborates his story. The nuclear industry in general is shedding a lot of staff, and employment prospects for those affected are not good, so that part of it rings true. We have been able to confirm directly that he and his wife, or former wife, are in the aftermath of a divorce, as papers have been filed with the local court which are in the public domain. Also, we have confirmed that they are living apart."

Khalid demurred, however. "If this is a trap, I would expect nothing less than all of this. If they're fishing for a substantial prize, then the bait would have to be good."

"I'm not disagreeing with you. I'm just setting out what we've done so far. It doesn't alter the nature of the risk."

"And what about the bait?" asked Khalid. "These sheets of irradiated uranium and molybdenum: how will we know that that's what they are when we seize them?"

"It will be possible to do a preliminary check on that," said Rahman. "There are types of Geiger counter that can identify the nature of a radioactive source from the pattern of radiation it emits, so it will be possible to do a quick check on each of the sheets to confirm that they are the genuine article. We know from independent sources that the Small Research Reactor at Sellafield is being used for this purpose. If this is a trap, and that's the point where the trap is to be sprung, then the outlook for Alan Southam at that moment would not be good."

"Much seems to depend on our assessment of Southam," observed Khalid.

"What was Mercury's impression of him?" asked Rahman.

"Mercury was cautiously inclined to regard him as genuine. Again, that just points in the same direction. It proves nothing."

Rahman asked: "Given that it's not immediately obvious how we might carry out this operation, would you have expected Alan Southam to have given a prompt as to the method, if this is a trap?"

"I wouldn't have expected it, no," said Saeed, "although the temptation to do so would be very great. But in the end, it wouldn't serve them any useful purpose. We would always hold the initiative. If this is a trap, then I'm confident that our people will be able to detect the signs, however small, of the preparations for it."

"What about his request to be brought out?"

Saeed shrugged. "That's what would be expected if his story were to be taken as genuine and coherent. I would agree with Southam that allowing us to get these items would be, for the UK and US, too high a price to pay just in order to plant a spy. If he was brought out, and our people carrying out the raid were intercepted, and either captured or destroyed, then that would put Southam in a situation of high risk. Our people would either use him as a hostage, or kill him. That's one reason why I'm inclined to doubt that this is a trap. The other reason is, why would the UK and US initiate such a scheme? If it's a trap, we will detect it in advance. We might even make use of it for our own ends – for example, deliberately springing the trap without trying to break into Sellafield."

"And if the purpose of it is to furnish a pretext for an attack on us? In other words, a pretext for war?"

"That's precisely what I meant just now about springing the trap. That doesn't mean that such an operation wouldn't still be risky; but if we held the initiative, we could assess the risk at each stage of the operation. But I think the greatest risk relates to the aftermath, which is the point you just made. Even if we were successful in seizing these items and bringing them back, we would have to maintain security procedures to keep our possession of the items secret indefinitely, in order to avoid justification for precisely such an attack on us, and that would be the greatest risk of the whole enterprise. Assessing that risk would be critical in deciding whether or not we went ahead with this operation."

The other two looked at Hamid Rahman.

"Not indefinitely," he said after a pause. "If we manage to reach the point where we have operational ballistic missiles with nuclear warheads, then at that point, our situation would change. Any large-scale attack on us after that point risks us making a nuclear response. After all, that's the main purpose of the military programme. The Americans think they have a right to attack, invade and overthrow the government of any small or medium-sized country they take a dislike to, regardless of international law. We have had to live with that threat for a long time now. One might have thought that their own experience in Vietnam, as well as the Soviet experience in Afghanistan, would have deterred the Americans from the folly of invading Afghanistan and then Iraq. But the Americans don't learn from history. Their massive preponderance in military power over any other country leads them to think that they can do whatever they want. In fact, this makes the United States a rogue state, from which much of the rest of the world is in danger. So, the incentive for us to carry out this operation is very great."

"I think that would be the main danger with this operation," said Khalid. "Even if it wasn't clear who was responsible for the raid, the Americans may just assume it was us and use that as a pretext for launching an attack on us anyway. Even if we managed to get these items back to this country, we wouldn't have time to do anything with them before the Americans launched a pre-emptive strike which destroyed our nuclear facilities. Unless there's an answer to that, then the whole purpose of this operation becomes invalid from the start."

"Well," said Rahman, "there is an answer, although I can't tell you very much about it in detail. Our nuclear sites which are often in the news because of the development of uranium enrichment facilities, are hailed by the Government to be for the legitimate purpose of civil nuclear power only. This is in fact now largely true. The military programme has been moved to a number of secret sites which, as well as being secret, are also proofed against nuclear attack. This means that an American attack against our known nuclear facilities would, in the first instance, create a political problem rather than a military one. How would the Government respond to such an attack?"

Saeed smiled and nodded. "I think I can see the elements of a plan beginning to fall into place," he said. "If it could be shown that the facilities attacked were indeed purely civil nuclear, such an attack would be outrageous. If, however, the international community continued to be hostile towards us despite this, then from an objective point of view, we would be entirely justified in developing nuclear weapons as our only effective defence against such attacks."

"If that were to be the plan," said Khalid, "it would still leave us with a difficult security situation. If the operation to seize these items involved the military in any way, then it would have to be a special operation of the highest security classification. That means that only those directly involved would know that it was a special operation, and of those, only a few trusted individuals would know what the operation was about. That would be difficult enough on its own. But it would also mean that the Government would be denying that the seizure was anything to do with this country, and might still be in ignorance of the truth if the Americans launched an immediate counter-strike against us. What their reaction would be when they discovered the truth, I don't know."

"Presumably it would have to involve the military," said Saeed. "The set of carrier frames would fill at least a medium-sized van, and together would weigh upwards of five hundred kilograms, to give you an idea of the size of the consignment. Only military special forces would have the ability to carry out a mission like that successfully. Given the distance involved, they would probably require support from the main military services. Can you think of any other way it could be done?"

"To answer that would require going into detail about how such an operation might be carried out," said Khalid. "Normally that would be assigned to a special task study within Special Operations; but that would mean involving people we don't know and can't vouch for, which basically rules that out. This particular mission is very location-specific, and it would be difficult if not impossible to disguise that. From a security point of view it would be ideal if we could agree a course of action just between the three of us. From an operational point of view that would be less than ideal because we wouldn't have the resources to check out the practicality of different options in detail. But if security about the operation is breached, then there will be no operation."

"I think it might be possible to rule out certain options on the basis of what we already know," said Saeed. "The carriers incorporate a certain amount of shielding, but they still emit radiation, mostly gamma, at well above background levels. A few minutes' exposure at close range isn't likely to be harmful, but anything much more than that would be undesirable. That rules out the idea of using commercial airlines to get the carriers back here. The carriers as they are would trigger radiation alarms at any airport. Packing them with enough shielding to block the radiation would make them immensely heavy, which would draw attention to them for that reason, if they were being considered for air freight.

"The alternative would be to use a private or chartered aircraft. The main problem there is the number of different sovereign airspaces the aircraft would have to pass through while news was breaking about the raid. This is even assuming it didn't have to land anywhere to refuel on the way. Presumably, if it was to have the range to make the flight non-stop with spare capacity to make a major detour if necessary, it would have to be something more substantial than a light aircraft or even a business jet. So we would still be talking about airliner-type aircraft and main airports, not small airfields or unofficial landing grounds in large fields."

"It's already starting to look like a seaborne operation," said Khalid. "That's what Alan Southam suggested, and presumably he has had time to give the matter some consideration."

"Which might mean it's part of a trap, of course," said Rahman.

"Is a seaborne operation any more viable than an airborne operation?" asked Saeed.

Khalid was thoughtful for a moment. "I'm fairly confident we could get a ship to a point off the south-west coast of Ireland without arousing any suspicion. In fact, in order to continue to avoid suspicion, it would have to proceed from there either east through the English Channel for London and ports in North-West Europe, north-east into the Irish Sea for Liverpool or Dublin, or north past Scotland for Scandinavia. So in fact we could get a ship to a point midway between Liverpool and Dublin. It would arouse suspicion if it didn't turn east or west at that point, but continued on towards the coast where Sellafield is located."

"What distance is it from that point to Sellafield?" asked Rahman.

"Mmm… a hundred and fifty kilometres maybe. Something like that. Say four and a half hours at twenty knots."

"Are there any ports nearer to Sellafield which might be a destination for the ship?"

"I don't think so – not for ocean-going ships. There may be one or two small ports, but as far as I know, nothing that would take an ocean-going ship – in other words, a minimum length of a hundred and fifty to two hundred metres. However, that's something to be checked out. Obviously, the nearer we could get a ship to Sellafield without arousing suspicion, the better."

"I think," said Saeed slowly, "that a seaborne operation is going to be the solution to this matter. I've just realised that what is needed for this operation is a decoy – a sort of grand decoy. And what you said just now about getting a ship as near to Sellafield as possible without arousing suspicion: I've had an idea that could be a solution to that also."

6

Robert Smith dropped into the chair in his office and clicked through his emails. He was unusual in that he still used an old-fashioned desk-top computer. The room he used as an office was set up as a proper office, with a proper desk, a proper office wall clock, a proper office wall calendar, and a proper office potted plant. He couldn't adjust to the idea of running his office entirely from a smart phone, in the way that young people did. Trying to juggle everything on a tiny screen was just too much hassle.

The phone rang. It was Sandor, from D Section of the Middle East Desk. He sounded in a good mood.

"Good morning. And how are we this morning?"

"It's Monday, so cut the crap."

"Oh well, there was no harm in trying."

"What do you want?"

"I want a little job doing in Ireland."

"What sort of little job?"

"A certain financial transaction has taken place there. I'd like the payee to be checked out. As much information as possible; but in particular, I need to know what the payment was for."

"And the other party in the transaction?"

"The Adversaries."

This was the name used for the country which was the main focus of D Section's activities. Any action by The Adversaries was normally assumed to be hostile.

"The money has moved from an account which they control, and which they still believe to be secret," Sandor continued. "In fact, we've hacked into it and have been monitoring it for several months."

"How urgent is this job?"

"It's fairly urgent. If they're up to something, then we need to keep pace with it. I don't want the trail to go cold."

"OK, but if it's a rush job, then you'll owe me one. I don't have people sitting around with nothing to do."

"I'm sure you don't, so your assistance will be very much appreciated."

"OK, let me have the details, and I'll keep you informed."

In the event, Smith decided to do the job himself. Even he could manage on a smart phone for a few days. It had been some time since he had last been to Ireland, and since his nearest investigative agent was in London, and already busy with another case, it seemed like a good opportunity to renew his acquaintance with the Emerald Isle. The job sounded straightforward enough. The payee in the transaction that Sandor wanted checking out was a Patrick Deasy, who was located, according to Sandor's information, in a small coastal town called Balbriggan, a few miles north of Dublin.

Smith's flight arrived in Dublin early evening. He checked in to a hotel at the airport, arranged a hire car for the following day, went down for dinner in the hotel restaurant, and retired to bed early. The following morning he ordered breakfast in his room, and as he ate, he looked through the file he had been sent about his quarry.

Patrick Deasy was a local businessman who had a number of different business interests. His main interest seemed to be a building company, Patrick Deasy and Sons of Balbriggan; but he also had a taxi business, a haulage company with half a dozen trucks, an inshore fishing business with a couple of fishing boats, and he was also involved in greyhound racing. He was 54, married with three sons, and lived at an address just outside Balbriggan. There was a phone number for the building firm. This wasn't bad for a file assembled at short notice. Apparently, Patrick Deasy had not previously been of any interest to the intelligence service.

The bedside phone rang. It was reception, calling to advise that his hire car had arrived. He finished his coffee and went downstairs. The car hire firm's representative was a young woman with a cheerful personality. It took a few minutes to complete the paperwork. She asked if he would mind dropping her off at her firm's office, which was a few hundred yards from the hotel. After dropping her off, he left the airport and joined the M1 motorway northbound. The M1 had only two lanes in each direction; but Ireland didn't have that much traffic.

Smith decided that he would be more or less upfront with Patrick Deasy about who he was, while being vague about exactly which department he worked for; with the only untruth being a claim that he was located at the Embassy in Dublin. The Embassy would back up his claim if they were questioned about it.

A few minutes later he came to the exit for Balbriggan. According to the file, Patrick Deasy's building firm was located on an industrial estate on the southern edge of the town. After a few minutes he found the industrial estate, turned into the entrance, and drove slowly round looking at each of the industrial units in turn. Patrick Deasy and Sons occupied a corner unit, behind which was a fenced compound containing stockpiles of building material. He parked and got out. Parked just in front of him was a patrol car of the Garda or police.

Inside the office at the front of the unit, there didn't seem to be anyone about. After waiting a couple of minutes at the reception desk, he rang the bell. When there was still no response, he rang again. Eventually a young man dressed in dark blue overalls appeared from a doorway at the back.

"Yes, can I help?" He looked rather harassed.

"I was hoping to speak to Mr Patrick Deasy if he's available. He wasn't expecting me."

The young man seemed to be taken aback by this.

"Mr Deasy... Oh... If you'll just excuse me a moment."

He disappeared back through the doorway. A minute later, another man appeared. This one was middle-aged, thickset, with thinning dark hair and a heavy, unsmiling face.

Smith looked at the man enquiringly. "Mr Deasy?" he asked.

The other regarded him for a moment. "You wished to speak with Mr Deasy: was it personal or business?"

"It's business, but he wasn't expecting me."

"I'm afraid Mr Deasy passed away on Sunday."

"Oh!" Smith's surprise was genuine. According to the file, Patrick Deasy was only 54. "I'm sorry to hear that. Had he been ill?"

"He died following what seems to have been an accident at one of his building sites. The matter is being investigated by the authorities."

As if to make the point, the Garda officer whose patrol car was parked outside appeared through the doorway at the back, to see what was going on.

"You were wanting to speak with Mr Deasy?" he asked.

"Yes, that's right."

"About what?"

"It was a business matter."

"If it has a bearing on the investigation into Mr Deasy's death, we may need to know the details. Do you have any identification?"

Smith produced his driving licence. "I'm afraid I can't discuss the nature of my business in public. If you need any information, it would have to be discussed in private."

The involvement of the Garda complicated matters. If they took an interest in his activities, that could hamper his freedom of action. A key piece of information that had to be protected was the bank transaction that was the cause of this enquiry. If The Adversaries once suspected that their account was compromised, it would shut off an important source of information. It had therefore been his intention to take the line that Patrick Deasy was thought to have had dealings with certain known individuals who were thought to be a security risk. He had been hoping that Patrick Deasy might have unwittingly volunteered information about the individuals he had dealt with, thus giving Smith the lead that he still needed. Now that Deasy was dead, he had to assess how much involving the Garda would be a help rather than a hindrance. He decided that, on balance, it would be a help, given that he no longer had a lead to follow. It might give him access to information not otherwise available without arousing suspicion.

"Can I speak to the officer in charge of the case?"

"Yes. He may want to speak to you anyway. If you'll wait here, please."

He produced a mobile phone from his pocket, and walked out of Smith's earshot whilst keying in a number. A few minutes later he was back.

"Superintendent Reilly will be here shortly. In the meantime you're to wait."

Smith sat down on a bench in the reception area to wait. The thought occurred to him that everyone in that place must be wondering about the near future. The people who worked there would be wondering about the future of the company, and whether they would still have jobs there for much longer. He was wondering how this investigation would pan out. At length, he heard a car arriving outside. A minute later, a uniformed Garda Superintendent walked in. He went straight through to the back of the premises without even glancing at Smith. After a couple of minutes, both the Garda officers returned to the reception area.

The Superintendent addressed Smith without preamble. "You were wanting to speak to Patrick Deasy about a business matter, I understand."

"That's right, yes."

"And your name is?"

Smith produced his driving licence again. "I'm only prepared to talk in private," he repeated.

"OK, we'll go out to the car."

He led the way to where he had parked his car, a big 4x4 adorned with the blue and yellow of the Garda. They got in, Smith in the front with Superintendent Reilly, who introduced himself by way of restarting the conversation.

Smith began by saying that he worked for the State Department, which was true in a loose sort of way; and that he was attached to the Embassy in Dublin, which was untrue, but he had the point covered. He then explained about The Adversaries, and the concerns about their nuclear programme, which Reilly was familiar with from news bulletins.

"We have information that Mr Deasy was contacted by agents of the regime who are known to us, and that he concluded some kind of business deal with them. The reason I'm here is to try and establish whether any such deal took place, and if so, what it was about. We need to keep track of anything the regime does overseas, especially when it's something out of the ordinary like this."

"I appreciate your concern, but I need to focus on factors relating to Mr Deasy's death."

"Are you able to say whether it was an accident or not?"

"We're still waiting for the report from the pathologist, so at the moment, I can't say."

"What was he doing at the building site on a Sunday afternoon?"

"We don't know, but that's also being investigated."

"If it turns out that Mr Deasy's death wasn't an accident, but something more sinister, then you'll have to give consideration to the possibility that agents of the regime were responsible."

Reilly was thoughtful for a moment. "I see. That would make the matter more complicated."

"If it came to that, we may be able to supply you with information, depending on its classification, that could assist your investigation. However, before that, I need to find out what Mr Deasy's connection with the regime was, and in particular, what was the nature of the business transaction that we think took place."

"Well, as far as that's concerned, you'll have to speak to the family's solicitor, who'll have taken charge of Mr Deasy's affairs until the inquest."

"What about his sons? If they're involved in the business, surely they would know."

"That might depend on whether this transaction involved the business. Also, this wouldn't exactly be the best time to approach members of the family about a business matter. It would be tactful to leave that for a week or two."

"I can't wait that long, I'm afraid. If some kind of transaction took place, it may be linked to an operation the regime is planning to carry out. If the transaction took place here, then it may mean that the operation will take place either here or elsewhere in Western Europe. If that is the case, then we definitely need to know about it, so we can't afford to let any potential leads go cold."

"Well, on your own head be it. Remember, you have no authority here, and if the family regard an approach by you so soon after Mr Deasy's death as an unwarranted intrusion, you risk a complaint being made to your Embassy."

"Perhaps if I were able to speak to the family's lawyer first, it wouldn't be necessary for me to approach the family. Can you give me the name of the lawyer?"

"Yes, that should be alright." Reilly reached behind the driver's seat and retrieved a folder. "It's a James Thomlinson of Harris and Bailey on Drogheda Street here in Balbriggan."

Smith wrote down the details.

"I hope you aren't intending to cause any trouble," Reilly said after a moment's pause.

Smith shook his head. "I've no intention of causing trouble. I've been sent here simply to gather information about what happened, or is thought to have happened. I don't have a remit to do any more than that."

"But if you find the information you're looking for, others may follow with a rather different remit."

"If you're talking about being suddenly confronted by the 101st Airborne on special operations, then forget it. Ireland isn't Panama or Grenada. We've always had good relations with Ireland, and no President would want to jeopardise that. At the moment, I've no idea what this business with Patrick Deasy may have been about. It may turn out to be of no consequence. If a major security problem is found on Irish territory, then it will be the Irish Government that will deal with it. We can offer assistance and support if you want it; but that would be up to your Government. If it turns out that Patrick Deasy's death wasn't accidental, then the business I'm investigating will presumably become a line of inquiry for you."

"That would depend on there being evidence linking the two. A police investigation isn't the same as an intelligence operation. If it turns out that you're right, my priority would be to apprehend those responsible for criminal offences, using evidence that would be required by a court to secure a conviction. Beyond that, the kind of things you're looking for wouldn't be directly relevant to me. However, that doesn't mean I wouldn't be interested in whatever you might find out."

"I shall bear that in mind."

He got out and returned to his car. There was a phone number for Harris and Bailey on the paper that Reilly had shown him. When he phoned the number, he was able to make an appointment to see James Thomlinson that afternoon. He then drove into the town centre.

He parked outside the offices of *The Balbriggan Enquirer* on Drogheda Street. The newspaper occupied several first-floor rooms which were reached by a flight of stairs up from the street door. He asked the young woman behind the reception window if he could speak to the reporter covering the Patrick Deasy story.

"Oh, I don't know if he's in – I'll just check," she said. "Who shall I say it is?"

Smith gave her the same information he had given to Reilly.

"Right," she said, as she took in what he had said. "I'll see if I can locate him."

She went to a desk at the back of the room and picked up the phone there. Because of the glass partition, her words were inaudible to Smith. Once or twice she glanced at him as she spoke.

At length, she returned to the window. "Mr Edwards is over at Drogheda at the moment, but he's coming back as soon as he can. He asked if you would wait. He shouldn't be long."

Smith nodded.

"Can I get you a coffee?"

"Thank you."

He sipped the coffee whilst looking at text messages on his phone. His daughter Zoë was asking if he would bring her something as a souvenir from Ireland. It was a brief glimpse of the real world intruding into the silly, desperate games that were the day-to-day of his life at work. He thought about what he might get for her. Waterford crystal? There would certainly be plenty of that in the duty-free shop at the airport.

There was the sound of someone coming up the stairs. The someone was a young man, slightly overweight and with sandy-coloured hair, and wearing a lightweight suit with no tie. He was a little out of breath from the stairs.

"Mr Smith?" he said, noticing the visitor.

They shook hands.

"Martin Edwards. Pleased to meet you. If you'd like to come through."

He let himself into the office, and Smith followed him through.

"If you'll just bear with me for half a minute while I file some copy. You've already met Fiona of course." He indicated the receptionist, who nodded.

He logged on to a computer, and took out his phone to do an upload. Task completed, he waved Smith through to another office.

"You'll understand," he said when they were seated, "my curiosity about why someone from the State Department is interested in the death of Patrick Deasy. You realise that he was just a local businessman. Well respected to be sure, but he operated very much in the local area. One or other of his wagons would do a run across the water to Britain from time to time, and maybe occasionally even to the Continent; but he was very far from being an international business tycoon."

"I don't doubt what you say; that was also my information. But there is, nevertheless, a reason for our interest." He explained as briefly as he could about The Adversaries and their nuclear programme.

"Our information is that an individual who had connections with the regime, and whom our intelligence people were keeping tabs on, recently contacted Mr Deasy. Since we had no information that Mr Deasy was involved in any kind of intelligence activity, we concluded that the contact may have related to some kind of commercial or business transaction. We thought it was unlikely that Mr Deasy would have been aware of the connections of the individual he was dealing with. The purpose of my inquiry is to find out what that transaction – assuming it took place – was about."

"And you don't have any indication or hint of what it might have been about?"

"Unfortunately not, no."

"You see, the point is that the economic crisis here in Ireland has hit almost all businesses badly, especially building firms, and Patrick Deasy's was no exception. In the last few months he was downsizing all his business operations, especially the building firm. He's had to pay off a lot of the workforce because, basically, building has stopped here in

Ireland since the collapse of the property bubble. He's also sold three of the wagons from his haulage company, the two fishing boats he owned, and he's put the taxi firm up for sale."

"Do you have any information about who may have bought any of these assets?"

"I know that one of the wagons was bought by a haulage company in Dublin; but as for the rest, I don't know. The taxi firm hasn't been sold yet, as far as I know."

"Anything else you know of?"

"In terms of tangible business assets, no. He was into greyhound racing as a hobby, but whether he'd sold any interests he'd had in racing dogs, I don't know."

"Are any of the sold assets still here, or do you know the whereabouts of any of them?"

"I know that one of the wagons was sold to Tolka Freight Transport. They have a large freight depot at Dublin docks, on the north side. I heard that one of the fishing boats was sold to a local fisherman." He paused for a moment. "You know, this is a hell of a story. You don't seem concerned about the idea of us splashing this across the front page of the *Enquirer*."

"That's because I'm confident that you won't do so."

"That we won't do so? What makes you think that? This is possibly the biggest story we've ever dealt with. Why wouldn't we run it?"

"Because I shall deny it. I shall deny that this conversation took place."

"But… what was the point of it, then? You asked to see me."

"Information. You've provided me with information that I wouldn't otherwise have been able to get, or at least, not nearly so quickly. And for that, I thank you."

"But if you are who you say you are, it mightn't be so easy to deny what your inquiries are about."

"That's what I'm trying to tell you. I actually work for the IRS – the Internal Revenue Service. My attachment to the State Department is simply because I sometimes work overseas. I was intending to speak to Mr Deasy about a business deal he was involved in which has incurred a tax liability in the States. He wanted to discuss a mutually agreeable way of settling the matter. What you've just told me will be of considerable help in my approach to the family lawyer who has charge of Mr Deasy's estate until the settlement of the will."

"You mean – all that you told me before is just a cock and bull story?"

"Oh, come on. Don't you think it sounded a tad far-fetched? A small-town Irish businessman getting involved in something like that?"

Edwards stared at him, weighing the thing up. Yes, of course it was far-fetched – on the face of it, it was little short of ludicrous. But there was a small voice inside him telling him that, for all that, it was not only believable, but the truth. Smith had misjudged his approach – he had been just a little too earnest for it to have been a charade.

"You know what? I don't believe that. I think that the first story you told me is the truth."

"But the point is, I shall deny it – deny that the conversation ever took place. So, I'm afraid you don't have a front page."

That was true, Edwards reflected, thinking about the situation. At least, it was true at the moment. However, if the first story were true, there was a possibility that there would be developments; and that could mean a front page, whether Smith wanted it or not.

After Smith left, Edwards stood up and walked over to the window and gazed pensively down into the street. After a few moments, Smith appeared on the street, having emerged from the street door. Smith got into a car parked on the street just below the newspaper offices. It was clearly a hire car. It was near enough for Edwards to be able to read the number plate. The journalist in him made him grab a pen and paper and jot it down.

Smith's visit to Harris and Bailey that afternoon was both short and unproductive. James Tomlinson was a young man, distinctly overweight, with a straggle of ginger fuzz around his chin that passed as a beard. After listening to what Smith had to say, he shook his head.

"I can appreciate your reasons for asking these questions, Mr Smith, but I'm afraid that it's out of the question that we should release any details about Mr Deasy's estate before the appointed time, which is after the reading of the will. Apart from any legal requirements, we also have the reputation of the firm to consider, which would be adversely affected if we were to breach the trust of one of our clients."

"Do you never have requests from the authorities, the police, to divulge information in such cases?"

"I'm not aware that we have in this firm. In any case, as a foreigner, you have no such authority here."

"Could you even confirm that a transaction took place?"

"I'm afraid I can give you no information at all, Mr Smith. Now, if you'll excuse me, I have an appointment with a client."

Back on the street, Smith returned to his car, and drove down to the harbour. He parked and got out, and strolled along the quayside towards the sea. The tide was in, and all the boats in the harbour were afloat: an untidy assortment of pleasure craft and trawlers. Most of the trawlers were alongside the quay, and on some of them there were signs of activity. He stopped by one of them, where an individual wearing the regulation woolly hat was tinkering with the trawler's deck winch.

"What do you catch mainly with this boat?" he asked.

Woolly Hat looked up from what he was doing, and grimaced. "Mostly EU regulations and fishing restrictions," he replied. "There's a lot more of them these days than fish in the sea. You wouldn't be an EU bureaucrat yourself, would you? You're dressed rather like one."

Smith gave a short laugh, realising how the lightweight business suit he was wearing might look to someone like Woolly Hat. "No, I'm from across the pond. I'm nothing to do with the EU. I'm over here in Ireland on a business trip, and I'm in Balbriggan because I was planning to meet with Mr Patrick Deasy to discuss a business matter. But I learned this morning that he died at the weekend, which was a bit of a shock."

"Yes, I heard about that. It was a bit of a shock. They say he had some sort of accident on the building site over at Coney Hill."

"He wasn't all that old, I believe."

"Early fifties, I think. It's not what you expect for someone of that age. But he had a lot of financial troubles after the recession started, and he had to sell off a lot of stuff to stay afloat financially. He had a couple of shrimpers, here at Balbriggan, and they were sold off."

"Shrimpers?"

"For trawling shrimps. They're quite small boats, with otter board trawls. They're both still here. One was bought by Joe Lenahan, who already had a couple of shrimpers. That's it over there. The other one was bought by some of our EU friends – Spaniards, I think. Spaniards or Portuguese. It's a trick that's becoming increasingly common. They buy up an Irish-registered boat, and that gives them the right to take a portion of Ireland's fishing quota in addition to their own country's. It's essentially a Spanish boat flying an Irish flag. The catch, and the money, go back to Spain, so Irish fishermen get less of their own quota as foreigners muscle in. It's largely one way, as there's very little in the other direction by Irish fishermen. It's one of the benefits of belonging to the EU."

"I see what you mean. You say the boat's still based here?"

"That's right. It's not here at the moment. They went out on yesterday's high tide. They've never landed a catch here, so they must be taking their catches to Spain. Although sometimes they're only away for a night or two – not long enough to get to Spain and back. But they've never landed a catch here, as far as I know."

"Maybe they land catches at other Irish ports."

"Maybe. But the fishing community here is fairly small, and we get to know what goes on soon enough."

"Just as a matter of interest, what would a boat like that set you back if you wanted to buy it?" Smith indicated the shrimper that Woolly Hat had pointed out.

"Well, I heard that Joe Lenahan paid about ninety thousand euros for it. That's just what I heard on the grapevine, mind."

Smith did a quick mental calculation, converting euros into dollars. It was close – pretty close.

A trawler… What the hell would they want with a trawler?

7

Alan Southam's next meeting with Mercury was more circumspect than the first. For communication, they used pay-as-you-go mobile phones, which, in Mercury's trade, were destroyed after each operation. This time, Mercury wanted Southam to check out a location to ensure there were no CCTV cameras there, or in the vicinity. After looking at a number of locations on Google Maps, Southam spent a couple of hours driving to the locations he had provisionally selected, to confirm the absence of CCTV. This done, he contacted Mercury with instructions, keeping the conversation as brief as possible.

They met a couple of days later. The location was a small gravel-surfaced car park next to a cemetery just off the A595, about a mile north of Beckermet. Mercury was to come dressed to blend in with the area, with woolly hat, sweatshirt, jeans and labourer's calf-length boots, and preferably with a couple of days' growth of beard. Southam was similarly attired. Southam bundled a few old clothes into a sack, which he brought with him. He arrived at the car park first, parking at the end furthest from the A595, and sideways on to it. Mercury arrived about a quarter of an hour later. He parked alongside, got out and climbed into the front passenger seat of Southam's car.

"I'm hoping," Southam said, "bearing in mind our previous conversation, that you will by now have a response to my request. If your people are seriously interested in this business, they must understand that the two go together. If I don't go back with them, then the deal's off. However, before you answer that, I thought you might like to have a look at the place I suggested in my proposal."

"I would be interested to see it in any event," Mercury replied enigmatically.

Southam started the engine, and turned right on leaving the car park, taking the narrow road that wound down the hill into the village of Beckermet. From the centre of the village he turned right up the hill onto the even narrower road that ran out to the village of Braystones, near the coast. He drove through the village and turned onto the lane that led to the railway station. At the station, the lane crossed the railway over a level crossing, beyond which it turned and descended via a long ramp onto the beach. Above the high tide line, along the top of the beach, the shingle formed an embankment, along which ran a rough trackway created by the passage of vehicles over a long period of time. Southam turned onto this going south, and driving at little more than walking pace. To their left on the landward side of the track, along the grassy foreshore above the shingle, was an irregular line of beach houses. These ranged from simple wooden huts to brick-built bungalows, some with low-walled gardens, most with a parking space for a car, some also with a boat or dinghy.

"Are these permanent residences?" Mercury asked.

"I think some of them are. Others are just for holiday use during the summer."

"It looks a bit Third World for this country. Given the weather here, it must be quite scary in a storm at high tide."

"I imagine it would be, yes. I'm not from this part of England, so I don't know too much about it. However, as you will see, these houses don't extend very far along, so they don't pose any threat of interference at the place where we're going."

They passed the last of the beach houses and continued slowly along the track. At length, they came to a point where the track gave way to an area of loose sand, and Southam pulled off the track onto the grass and parked the car.

"We'll have to walk from here," he said. "Beyond here it's not suitable for ordinary cars, only four-wheel-drive vehicles. However, first I want you to look at the river."

They walked across the strip of coarse turf on the landward side of the track, and from the top of the embankment, they could look down onto the River Ehen.

"As you can see," said Southam, "the river flows roughly parallel to the coast, creating a long spit of land which forms the coast along here, all the way down to Sellafield. The end of the spit is at Sellafield, where the river turns and finally flows into the sea. If you look to your left, the railway bridge there is the last link between this spit and the mainland, before the bridge which carries the waste discharge pipes across the river at Sellafield; so if your people were holding the bridge at Sellafield, getting access to that place would be quite difficult for the British authorities, especially if they were aware that they were facing armed opposition."

"And crossing the river?"

"Well, look for yourself. It's like this all the way down."

They stood looking down at the River Ehen, which was a turgid brown flood about 100 feet wide.

"If they ran a train up from Sellafield to that bridge, they could be on the spit fairly quickly."

"They couldn't do that because your people would be blocking the railway at the bridge at Sellafield. Any train would therefore have to come from the north, which would mean Whitehaven at the nearest, and probably further away than that. In the small hours of the night, that would take time to organise. And there would be confusion: to begin with, the British would not be sure what was happening, and they would have no information about the military situation. That's why surprise and speed would be your main advantage. You would be in and out before the British had even begun to react."

Mercury nodded slowly. "OK, yes, I see."

They continued walking south. Southam had the sack he had brought slung over his shoulder to add some local colour to his appearance. As they approached the bridge carrying the waste discharge pipes, now clearly visible, Mercury produced his mobile phone and began taking pictures. At one point he walked to the top of the embankment to take pictures of the river. As they got close to the bridge, he stopped, looking at it carefully.

"Are you sure there are no CCTV cameras on that structure?" he asked.

"As sure as I can be. I had a good look, including with binoculars, when I was down here a few days ago, and I couldn't see any."

They walked up to the fence which formed the compound surrounding the seaward end of the bridge. Slowly, they walked round it, with Mercury continuing to take pictures. Finally, Mercury stood looking up at the bridge from the riverbank just to the south of it.

"OK, I've seen enough. We can start back now."

They started walking back towards where they had left the car.

After a couple of minutes, Mercury spoke again. "Now that I've seen the place for myself, and am satisfied that it is as you described it, I can tell you that the people I represent have accepted your proposal. That includes, as you requested, a job as an engineer in our civil nuclear industry, and being taken back by the raiding party. In fact, that would also be one of the conditions on our side: a sort of insurance policy, if you like, as I'm sure you'll understand."

"Of course, I entirely understand."

Underneath, Southam was elated. What had started off as a long shot, perhaps a very long shot, was now a lifeboat – the only one available. That same week, he had been advised by his solicitor that his ex-wife was going back to the courts to try and seize more of what was left of his income and assets – she already had the house – and he was facing financial ruin, even before losing his job. Now, he had the prospect of a new job as a nuclear engineer, and an exit to a place where he would be beyond the reach of any British or European court. One further matter remained, however.

"One other thing. If I were to transfer the money in my bank account to one of your country's banks, would it be beyond the reach of any British attempt to sequestrate it?"

Mercury had been expecting the question. "It would, yes. But before you do that, you should understand the implications of it. The West has managed to seal off and isolate our financial institutions from most of the rest of the world. This means that direct transfers of money into or out of our banks across our frontiers are now effectively blocked. Most of our assets outside our frontiers have been frozen or confiscated.

"So, in the first instance, it will not be possible for you simply to move your money into one of our banks. Apart from the West's blockade, there are, obviously, also security considerations. Any movement of money in from outside might be a Trojan horse from the West, trying to find secret channels by which we get round their blockade. Such channels exist, but because we protect them with security measures, it wouldn't be possible for you simply to move your money into one of our banks.

"Instead, we have a series of quarantined accounts which exist outside our frontiers. The West knows that we have such accounts somewhere, but because we also protect these accounts with security measures, they have not so far discovered them. We would give you instructions about where to put your money initially. You would have to give our people the power to move the money on at their discretion into one of these quarantined accounts. It would have to stay there untouched until it was given security clearance to be transferred to a bank inside our frontiers. That's the procedure you would have to follow. During the time it was in the quarantined account, you would not have access to your money.

"There is one other point I should mention, which may already have occurred to you. If you were taken away at gunpoint by the raiding party, it would look as if you were simply a victim of the raid, being taken as a hostage or something like that. However, if you empty your bank account at around the same time, even if it isn't clear where the money has gone, that will inevitably raise suspicions about your involvement in the raid."

"That had occurred to me, yes. But it's a risk I'm prepared to take. How long would the money have to stay in the quarantined account?"

"There isn't a set period – it depends on the security situation of the individual case, so I can't say. But you would be receiving a salary, so you wouldn't be destitute."

Mercury hadn't quite understood his meaning; but it was of no consequence. It amounted to a choice between a possibility that he would keep the money he had earned, and a near certainty that he would lose it all. For the time being, at least, he was content.

8

As they came abeam of the Langness light, Ahmed lowered the binoculars through which he had been studying the lighthouse on its rocky peninsula, and swung the wheel gently, bringing the *Maid of Cork* round onto a new course, heading due north-east. He held the wheel steady for a minute, then updated the log, before stepping out of the wheelhouse.

"That's it – we're on the run in," he shouted, raising his voice above the noise of the engine.

The two men out on the fish deck, Mehmed and Ali, both nodded. Ahmed secured the wheel, then joined them to help as they prepared for a trawl run. Mehmed released the winches and paid out some trawl line from both winches. Ahmed and Ali checked the lines to make sure they were secure and running freely through the blocks, then pulled the two drogues into place and attached them to the lines. They then held the drogues out over the side of the boat, and, at a nod from Mehmed, released them into the sea. Mehmed let the winches pay out the lines slowly, checking that the drogues were smoothly under tow. Ahmed stepped back into the wheelhouse and gradually opened the throttle of the engine to counter the pull of the drogues. Running with drogues was a lot simpler than with nets, and once the drogues were over the side and under water, there was no way of telling that they were not trawling with nets.

Ahmed gradually increased the engine revolutions to give the boat sufficient way against the drogues. Above the roar of the engine could now be heard, or rather felt through the deck, the vibration from the propeller, which was making a tremendous racket. He carefully annotated the log, recording course, position and time. Gathering this information in the log was an important part of the run.

They were now running between the Isle of Man, to port, and the Cumbrian coast, ahead and to starboard, and Ahmed studied both coastlines through the binoculars. Off their starboard beam, about ten miles distant, was a large cluster of wind turbines of an offshore wind farm. This posed a navigation hazard, and its position had to be charted exactly. On this run, they were going to swing much further east than on previous runs, and Ahmed held the *Maid of Cork* on a steady north-easterly course as she bored straight towards the Cumbrian coast.

He carefully watched the readings from their radar. Their exact position in this area was of some significance. They were in waters which were part of the UK's economic zone. As a fishing boat from an EU member state, they needed a licence from the UK Fisheries Department to fish there, and were therefore at risk of being stopped to confirm that they had a licence. It would be even more awkward if they were stopped and forced to reveal that they were running with drogues and not nets. That was a calculated risk: they would be more likely to arouse suspicion if they just cruised around without apparently attempting to fish at all. It would only be if they were to land catches on a dockside that they would be at risk of breaking the quota attached to that particular vessel. As they had not landed any catches, that wasn't an immediate problem. Eventually, however, questions would be asked about why they were apparently making regular fishing trips without landing any catches; but hopefully, this business would be completed long before then.

They would be at much higher risk of being stopped if they crossed the 12 nautical mile limit of the UK's territorial waters, and this was Ahmed's main concern now, watching the radar returns as they approached the Cumbrian coast. Looking through the binoculars again, he focused on the coast straight ahead. The coast along here seemed to be formed mostly of low sand dunes covered in coarse grass, occasionally rising into low bluffs. More detail emerged in the binoculars as they got closer. The two objects on the coast ahead gradually materialised into what looked like radar towers, rising above the sand dunes. They marked the location of the Eskmeals test range, which, on their present course, they were heading straight towards. The radar was probably used for tracking shot from the range, but Ahmed assumed that it very likely had other purposes as well. Watching me, watching you...

To the south of Eskmeals, the land rose steeply from the coast to the summit of a broad, round-topped mountain, which according to Ahmed's map was called Black Combe. At that distance, its rounded silhouette was grey rather than black. To the north, the fringe of grass-covered sand dunes extended into the distance, broken only by the estuary just north of Eskmeals.

By the time this amount of detail was visible in the binoculars, the *Maid of Cork* was within 15 nautical miles of the coast. Ahmed noted the position in the log, then swung the wheel gently to start bringing the boat round onto a new course. They could only turn slowly whilst towing the drogues, and by the time they had settled onto the new course, now running parallel with the coast, the distance had reduced to less than 13 nautical miles. This was the nearest they could safely approach.

After updating the log, Ahmed resumed his study of the coast through the binoculars. They were now abeam of a coastal settlement: Seascale, according to the map. Looking at what he could see of it, Ahmed noted that this was where the railway re-emerged into view from seaward, its course indicated by the embankment along which it ran. North of Seascale, it was more or less continuously in view, running close to the foreshore, mostly along embankments.

A few minutes later, they started to draw level with Sellafield. Observing from sea level, it was only possible to see the seaward end of the site; but Ahmed noted the bridge that carried the waste discharge pipes out of the site and down onto the beach. There seemed to be quite a number of cranes clustered further inland, suggesting that building work was ongoing.

There was only time for a brief look at Sellafield, however. The territorial waters around St Bees Head and the Point of Ayre were rapidly converging ahead. Ahmed leaned out of the wheelhouse and shouted for the other two. He throttled the engine back to reduce the pull on the trawl lines as Mehmed started the winches hauling in the drogues. A few minutes later, the drogues were at the surface alongside, and Ahmed and Ali hauled them over the sides and onto the deck. The trawl lines were unfastened, and they folded the drogues up for stowage.

At that moment, Mehmed gave a shout and pointed. Simultaneously, there was a sudden roar as an aircraft flew directly over the boat, barely 100 feet up. Ahmed dashed into the wheelhouse and grabbed the binoculars, quickly noting the time by his watch as he did so. With some difficulty he managed to focus the binoculars on the aircraft, which was now turning to starboard, moving fast. It was banking quite steeply as it turned, giving Ahmed a good view of it for several seconds. It was a twin-engined plane, propeller-driven, with straight wings, set low, and a high-set tailplane. It looked like a twin-engined light aircraft, perhaps a business or executive aircraft. The engines sounded like turboprops rather than piston engines. Having completed its turn, it was now coming straight at them again, and seconds later it made another low pass right over them.

Ahmed had a brief view of the underside of the aircraft before it was past them and receding rapidly, turning as it went. The light was good enough for him to see that it was a uniform grey in colour, and devoid of any identification markings that he could see. A civilian aircraft would have had its registration letters on the underside of one wing, which he would have been able to see, had they been there. It was therefore a military aircraft, albeit one which was not obviously a military type.

Ahmed pushed the engine throttle over to maximum revolutions, and then swung the wheel, making a sharp turn to port. The engine responded with a roar of noise as the *Maid of Cork* heeled sharply to port as it made the turn – Mehmed and Ali had to hang on to the starboard gunwale to keep their balance. Ahmed held the wheel over until the Isle of Man was off their starboard beam, before straightening the boat on its new course. They were now headed south-west, and as the boat picked up speed, Ahmed studied the map. They were about 14 nautical miles east of the Manx coast, and steering a course running roughly parallel with it. Ahmed watched the radar returns to make sure they didn't get too close to the coast.

After quickly updating the log, he looked round for the aircraft. He spotted it astern, apparently turning slowly as it flew. It was evidently now circling them at a distance of about half a mile. Looking at the map, he saw that they had nearly 30 miles to go to reach the Irish economic zone. Going flat out, that would take about an hour and fifty-five minutes, if they could maintain that speed. He looked at the aircraft again. It was still circling: they had undoubtedly attracted unwelcome attention. It looked as if it was keeping track of them to assist their interception by a surface vessel. However, such a vessel would have to be fast if it was to catch them before they reached Irish waters. Realistically, the vessel would have to come from Douglas if it was to catch them, which would mean a stern chase. A vessel from Barrow in Furness would have to be capable of well over 40 knots to have any chance of intercepting them. The only permanent Royal Navy presence in the Irish Sea was a patrol boat at Liverpool, which was too far away.

Ahmed switched the setting of the radar to a 360 degree sweep to see what other vessels were around. The nearest were two other trawlers about 10 miles south-south-east of them, which he could see himself. A view through the binoculars confirmed that they were trawlers. To the east, there was a confused clutter of returns from the wind turbines off Barrow in Furness. There were two large vessels beyond visual range to the south-east, in Liverpool Bay. After watching for a few minutes, he could see that neither of them was moving in his direction. One was moving towards Liverpool, and the other was moving more or less due west. They were probably passenger ferries. There was nothing to the north of them: no sign of any pursuit from Douglas.

He checked the distance to the Manx coast again. The distance had increased slightly since he last checked, as the coast was now trending more to the west. He adjusted course to keep level with the coast, then eased back the throttle on the engine. There was no point in hammering the engine needlessly if there was no sign of a pursuit. He updated the log, secured the wheel, and stepped out of the wheelhouse to speak with the other two.

After discussing the situation, they decided to prepare for another trawl run, this time with nets instead of drogues, for the sake of appearances. The nets were broken out and attached to the trawl lines on each side of the deck, preparatory to being hauled out over the sides of the boat. Mehmed checked the trawl lines through the blocks, then paid out some line from each of the winches.

Ahmed looked round for the aircraft. He couldn't see it. Puzzled, he carefully quartered the sky, but still couldn't find it. He stepped back into the wheelhouse and studied the radar. He watched several sweeps of the radar, which showed no trace of it. He adjusted the sweep for height, and finally spotted the aircraft well to the east of them. It was much higher than it had been before – at least five or six thousand feet – and now nearly 10 miles away.

He might have puzzled for longer about what the aircraft might be up to, but there was an alarm bell ringing at the back of his mind. Something about the previous screen. He switched back to the previous setting. He had been so intent on looking for the aircraft that he had almost missed it. There was a ghost echo to the west of the cluster of returns from the wind turbines off Barrow in Furness. He cursed under his breath as he adjusted the radar, trying to get a clearer image, but radar clutter from the wind turbines was making it difficult. This was a possibility he had overlooked. There were evidently other hazards associated with the wind turbines.

The best image he could get seemed to indicate that it was about 15 miles away. It was moving quite fast – maybe as much as 25 knots. He watched it through several sweeps of the radar, trying to plot its course. At length, he managed to get a bearing. He plotted it on the map, marking off positions based on its approximate speed. On a rough calculation, it would reach the last plotted position, where it would cross their own projected course, in about fifty-five minutes. At their present speed, they would reach the same position at about the same time. It was coming for them.

He cursed softly again, and pushed the engine throttle over to maximum revolutions. He quickly updated the log, then picked up the binoculars. After a minute, he found it. It was still too far away to see clearly, but he could see a prominent bow wave, indicating that it was moving fast.

He stepped out of the wheelhouse. Mehmed looked at him inquiringly.

"We've got company," Ahmed said in response. He handed Mehmed the binoculars and pointed. Mehmed studied the other vessel for a couple of minutes.

"Will they catch us?" he asked. He handed the binoculars to Ali so he could look.

"Not sure. I think they would have done if we'd stayed at the speed we were going, but I've just increased speed to maximum power. If they change course, it means they've noticed that; but whether they can catch us now might depend on whether they've got any extra speed themselves."

"We could dump stuff to lighten the boat." Mehmed indicated the nets and trawl lines.

Ahmed shook his head. "That'd be an indication that we were up to no good. It'd be less risky to rely on bluff. If we manage to beat them to Irish waters, we might actually start a trawl run, just for the sake of appearances."

He stepped back into the wheelhouse and looked at the radar screen. They had drifted out from the Manx coast a little, so he made a slight course correction, to a more westerly course. He checked their speed, did a position check, then checked their course. He calculated that they would reach Irish waters in just forty minutes.

He watched the other vessel through several sweeps of the radar, in order to plot its course and speed. This confirmed that the other vessel had changed course since he last checked, clearly in response to the *Maid of Cork*'s increase in speed. It looked as if the other vessel had also increased its speed slightly. Would it be enough? He plotted a course projection. His first calculation was that the other vessel would reach the same point at the edge of Irish waters in forty-one minutes. He checked the readings again: a second calculation gave forty-two minutes. It was going to be close: a matter of a minute or so, and a few hundred metres.

He was updating the log when a sudden roar made him look up. The aircraft was back. He secured the wheel and went out on deck. The aircraft had flown right over them, and was now off their starboard beam, flying low, and already turning. They watched as the turn continued. It looked as if the aircraft was circling them as before. However, after completing three-quarters of a circle, it turned sharply and flew towards them. It came at them from dead ahead, flying very low, and passing over the boat at a height of barely 50 feet. It was so low that they felt the wind of its passage as they stood on the deck. It climbed away, turned and flew a half-circle until it was dead ahead of them, and then turned sharply to make another low pass over the boat.

Ahmed said suddenly, "Don't look at the plane. Look as if you're busy with the nets."

He squatted down and started pulling at one of the nets, as if he was checking the floats and weights. The others did likewise, as the aircraft again roared overhead at less than 50 feet. Again, it climbed and circled to make another pass.

"It's almost as if they're trying to attract our attention," observed Mehmed with a grin. "They must be bombarding us with radio messages." The radio was switched off.

"The radio is currently undergoing maintenance. I've removed a circuit board for inspection – at least, I will do in the next few minutes."

They continued attending to the nets as the aircraft made another pass. Ahmed then stood up, retrieved the binoculars and went into the wheelhouse. A check on the radar showed that the distance to the Manx coast now allowed a further course correction to a more westerly direction. Each of these course corrections made the other vessel's pursuit more of a stern chase, which was to their advantage. He looked at the engine rev counter. The engine seemed to be holding steady on maximum revolutions. If they lost the race, it wouldn't be for want of trying.

He picked up the binoculars and looked at the other vessel. It was now close enough for him to see that it had a broad bridge or superstructure across nearly the full width of the vessel. It was almost certainly a Royal Navy patrol boat, which would normally be based in Liverpool. It was just bad luck that it must have been at Barrow in Furness that day. He cast an eye over the boat to see if anything was amiss in the event that they were intercepted and boarded, but everything seemed as it should be. Mehmed and Ali were diligently attending to the nets on the deck, while the aircraft continued to make low passes over the boat.

As Mehmed had suggested, they were probably being bombarded with radio messages by the patrol boat and the aircraft, demanding that they heave-to until the patrol boat could catch them up. He located a screwdriver and took the cover off the radio. He knew little about radios or electronics, and not wanting to damage the radio, he confined himself to unscrewing a couple of wires, leaving the ends in mid-air. It was enough to look convincing.

There was little else to do but wait to see who won the race. The aircraft had stopped making passes over them and was now circling them at a distance of about half a mile as before. Ahmed started to do position checks. They were now just under 2 miles from Irish waters. The other vessel was just over 4 miles away – close enough for him to plot a clear bearing and speed. It was doing 26 knots – almost twice their speed, even on maximum revolutions. It was still on a slightly converging course, which gave it an additional marginal advantage. They would reach Irish waters in just over eight minutes. The other vessel would reach the same point in nine minutes.

As he did further position checks, however, Ahmed noticed that the other vessel had increased its speed slightly. They were evidently wringing the last ounce of power out of their engine. A further check showed that this cut the margin to almost nothing. However, there was now scope for a further slight course correction, making their course now almost due west. The other vessel was now more or less dead astern, making it a straight stern chase. He looked ahead to the imaginary line on the water that was their objective. Mehmed and Ali were leaning over the port gunwale looking aft, watching the pursuing vessel. A final position check indicated that they were just going to make it. He watched their position as he counted down the distance – five hundred metres; two hundred; one hundred.

When they crossed the line, the other vessel was about four hundred metres behind them. By this time, it was clearly visible even without binoculars. The hull and the broad superstructure, topped by a multi-windowed bridge, were painted a uniform pale grey colour. He could see a couple of people moving about on the vessel's foredeck. Looking through the binoculars at the vessel's bridge, he was somewhat startled to find himself looking directly into the face of an individual who at that moment was also studying him through binoculars. Above the binoculars was a Royal Navy white peaked cap, leaving no doubt about the identity of their pursuers.

Ahmed watched with interest to see what the other vessel would do now that it had failed to beat them to Irish waters. Since there was no other vessel in the vicinity, there was nothing they could do to stop the British from boarding the *Maid of Cork*, even though it would cause a diplomatic incident. However, even as these thoughts ran through his head, he saw the bow wave of the other vessel diminish and fade away as it rapidly lost speed. It started to turn as it did so, until it was running parallel with the boundary line between British and Irish waters, just on the British side of it. They knew exactly where they were. Ahmed throttled the engine back, but maintained course. This meant that the distance between the two vessels now started to increase, so having secured the wheel and updated the log, Ahmed went out onto the fish deck.

"We'll do a trawl run, just to make things look authentic for our British friends," he said.

Mehmed went forward to the winches, and Ahmed and Ali finished preparing the nets and moved them into position. The sun came out from behind a bank of cloud. It was turning out to be quite a pleasant day.

9

Superintendent Reilly of the Dublin Garda looked up from the report he was reading as the buzzer on his desk phone sounded. He picked the receiver up.

"Reilly."

"James Mahony, sir. I wouldn't normally have troubled you with a matter of this sort, but I thought you might be interested in this case. I've a young woman here from a car hire firm at the airport who's reporting that one of their cars is missing. It's overdue for return, but the guy who hired it isn't answering his phone, and he hasn't returned to his hotel. She's been round there and checked. The guy's an American named Robert Smith."

"I see," Reilly said slowly. "Can you bring her up, James?"

A couple of minutes later, Garda Mahony ushered in the young woman, whom he introduced as Julia Malone. She came across as intelligent and competent, which made things easier.

"The car was due to be returned yesterday," she said. "When it hadn't been returned by the end of the day, it was registered as overdue. Normally, we don't have a problem if someone wants to extend a hire period, even if they do it over the phone from wherever they are; but we haven't heard from Mr Smith since we delivered the car to him last week. When we phoned him, we just got the phone's message service. We left a message, but there hasn't been any response. He was staying at a hotel at the airport. I went round there this morning, but he wasn't there. The hotel staff said that he was due to have checked out this morning; but apparently he hasn't been seen at the hotel for some days. He hasn't checked out, and they said that some of his belongings are still in his room.

"He hasn't paid his bill, although I expect they'll take the money off his card. We took payment in advance for the car hire, but obviously we're now concerned about the car. I don't know whether the guy's just done a bunk, or something untoward has happened; but in any event, we decided we needed to notify you."

Reilly nodded, and was thoughtful for a moment. "Did you speak to Mr Smith yourself when he hired the car?"

"Yes, I delivered the car to him at the hotel. He's an American – he gave his contact address as their Embassy in Dublin."

"Did he say anything to you about what he was doing here in Ireland?"

She shook her head. "No, not really. He said he was over here on a business trip for a few days, but nothing specific."

"Hmm. Do your cars have tracking devices fitted?"

Again, she shook her head. "I know that such things are available, but we also have to consider the views of our customers, many of whom would regard such a thing as an unacceptable intrusion into their privacy. In any case, if we lose a car, it's covered by the insurance, which is built into the hire price, so it's just a normal business risk. It's still not good to lose a car, which is why we're concerned in this case."

"Have you notified the Embassy of the fact that Mr Smith has gone missing?"

"Not yet. Because he's presumably a foreign diplomat, I wanted to ask you about contacting the Embassy before we do so."

Reilly nodded. "You should contact the Embassy to inform them that Mr Smith and the car have apparently gone missing, and also that you've informed us, and that we're investigating the matter. I presume you've given Garda Mahony the relevant details about the car."

"Yes, and copies of the paperwork raised when Mr Smith hired the car."

"Good. You've been very helpful, Mrs Malone, and I appreciate that. Garda Mahony will be your point of contact in the first instance; but I don't doubt that you'll be hearing from me again."

After they had left the room, Reilly was thoughtful for a minute, then picked up the phone again and dialled the switchboard.

"Can you put me through to the Special Detective Unit please – extension 26991."

He waited while the call was put through. It was answered almost immediately.

"Liam Powers."

"It's Kevin Reilly. Do you remember the American I told you about who was sniffing around the Deasy case?"

"Robert Smith?"

"Yes. Well – it looks as if he's gone missing. We've just been contacted by a car hire firm who say that the car he hired hasn't been returned and is now overdue. He's apparently gone missing from his hotel without checking out, and leaving his belongings behind."

Liam Powers was silent for a moment. "I'll be right over," he said.

Detective Superintendent Liam Powers scrolled through the pages of the report slowly as he read through it again. He was sitting at the spare computer terminal in Reilly's office.

"This is the latest?" he asked at length.

Reilly nodded.

"The pathologist was clear that Patrick Deasy died as a result of injuries caused by the fall from the scaffolding. There was no other cause of death. So, we're back to asking what was he doing on the scaffolding, given that it was a Sunday afternoon and no work was going on? And how did he come to fall? We made a detailed examination of the scaffolding and planking immediately above where he fell for any sign of a struggle or fight, but the results of that were inconclusive. At that point, we would normally have come to a provisional conclusion that it was either an accident, or possibly suicide, given that there's no evidence of foul play. We've taken swabs for traces of DNA, but normally they would just be for the record, in case there were any future developments.

"However, because of the story told to us by Robert Smith, potentially, these have taken on additional significance. At the moment, we're still awaiting the results of the analysis from Forensics. I phoned them just after I phoned you, but the results are still not available. I say 'potentially' because, frankly, I didn't know what to make of the story this character told me. I passed it on to you as a matter of routine; but if it turns out that Patrick Deasy's death didn't involve foul play, then it wouldn't be my query."

"Unless Robert Smith's disappearance does involve foul play."

Reilly nodded. "Depending on what else was involved, of course. If it was primarily an intelligence matter, I probably wouldn't get a look-in. What did you make of it?"

"At the moment, the problem is lack of information. We don't know anything about this financial transaction that Smith talked about, so we don't know exactly what he was looking for. I arranged for someone to phone the Embassy and ask to speak to Robert Smith. They said he wasn't available at that moment, and asked for a contact number so he could phone back. That effectively established his bona fides to that extent. You didn't ask about the sale of assets by Patrick Deasy when you interviewed members of the family?"

"Not in this connection, no. The interviews took place before I spoke to Robert Smith. The interviews were difficult, but they didn't give any indication of foul play. If Smith had come up with something specific, we could have judged it on the detail; but basically, he was just fishing for information. The indications were all pointing towards either suicide or an accident, and at that point I wasn't convinced of the need to put the family through the stress of further interviews on the basis of an unsubstantiated story of that sort."

"But if Smith has gone missing under suspicious circumstances, then the situation would be different."

"Yes. In that case, there would be two aspects to it, as I see it. The first would be to find out what had happened to Smith, and as part of that, whether there was anything in this case he said he was investigating; the second would be to establish whether there was any link between that and the Deasy case."

"If Smith has gone missing, we'll need to speak to members of the Deasy family again as soon as possible, to see if there's anything in this story about a financial transaction."

"I'll see if I can set that up today. Looking at it now, with hindsight, I was probably remiss in not doing that earlier. But when I spoke to Smith, I had great difficulty in taking him seriously. My impression of him was that he was probably some kind of conman up to no good; but there wasn't much I could do about it at that point."

"Your impression may not have been all that far off the mark. Some of the best conmen in the business are spies."

Robert Smith's hire car was found the following day, parked in the car park next to the harbour in Balbriggan. The car was locked, but it appeared to be intact and undamaged. A parking ticket indicated that it had been there for three days. Reilly and Powers arrived on the scene within a few minutes of each other. An incident van and two other Garda vehicles had already arrived, and the area immediately around Smith's car was being cordoned off. The car was being examined and photographed from various angles.

Garda Mahony greeted Reilly on his arrival. "It's fortunate that Balbriggan isn't such a big place. I was also lucky quite quickly. This was an obvious place to look. I've contacted Julia Malone at the car hire firm, and she's on her way over with the key."

Liam Powers joined them, having just arrived and parked his car. They waited while a sniffer dog was used to check Smith's car for traces of explosives; but the dog gave no reaction. They looked through the windows of the car, but nothing of any interest was visible. A few minutes later, Julia Malone arrived, and was waved through on Reilly's instructions.

"Well, that was quick," she said. "And there doesn't look to be anything wrong with it."

"Even so, it might not be the best outcome from your point of view," said Reilly. "Robert Smith is now the subject of an investigation, and I'm afraid we'll have to retain the car, at least for the time being. You will get it back, intact and undamaged, assuming there's nothing wrong with it now; but it means you won't have the use of it in the interim."

She shrugged. "I'm relieved that the car's been recovered intact. We have to be prepared for cars going out of service occasionally for one reason or another, so we'll cope with that. Have you located Mr Smith?"

"No, not yet. This development means that the matter has become more complicated, and potentially more serious. The first thing we need to do is look in the boot, if you've got the key."

"Yes, of course."

She watched as Reilly pulled on a pair of latex gloves, suddenly understanding what he meant. They all then stood clear and took cover. She pressed the key fob, unlocking the car. After waiting for a few moments, Reilly walked over to the car. She decided not to look as he cautiously opened the boot. The boot was empty, however, apart from a small toolkit at the back. Carefully, Reilly lifted the floor shelf to check that there was nothing underneath other than the spare wheel. He closed the boot, walked round and opened the driver's door. After a careful look, he reached in to pull the bonnet release catch. He propped the bonnet up on its rest and checked the engine bay.

"If you'll let me have the key," he said.

She walked over and handed him the key before walking back again.

Reilly looked to check that the handbrake was on and the gearstick in neutral, pushed the key into the ignition and turned it. The engine started straight away.

"Sounds alright."

He let it run for a minute before switching it off. He walked round and closed the bonnet.

"Right, that's fine," he said. "If you'll go over to the incident van with Garda Mahony, he'll give you a receipt and other documents for the car while it's in our custody. We'll need to take fingerprints from anyone at your firm who may have been in contact with the car, to exclude them from our inquiry. The prints will all be destroyed at the end of the inquiry. Garda Mahony will be dealing with that. I appreciate your help, Mrs Malone, and for coming over so quickly."

She smiled and nodded, then walked towards the incident van with Garda Mahony.

Liam Powers waited until she was out of earshot.

"I've hooked a fish," he announced.

Reilly looked at him inquiringly.

"My agent phoned the Embassy again this morning, asking to speak to Robert Smith. The first call followed the same routine as before: he was asked to leave his name and phone number so that Smith could call back when he was available. A short while later, there was a call back. It wasn't Smith, but someone at the Embassy who wouldn't identify himself. He asked my agent what he wanted to speak to Smith about. My agent said that he had some information for Smith, but it was for Smith's ears only. He asked again if Smith was available to speak to, and when the answer was negative, he hung up.

"A short while after that, there was a further phone call, this time from someone calling himself Michael Garcia. Mr Garcia was extremely insistent that my agent tell him the information he had for Smith, when and where he last saw and spoke to Smith, and his current location. My agent again asked if Smith was available to speak to, and when the answer was again negative, he hung up. The Embassy called back three times after that, but on my instructions, my agent didn't answer the calls. They'll already know from other sources – the car hire company – that Smith's gone missing. They must be in something of a flap by now. They'll be more amenable the next time they come back. I can play them like a fish on a line."

"You should maybe be careful – it's a fish with rather large teeth."

"I know what I'm doing. It's one of the games that we play. They're on my patch, so they're at a disadvantage. They will have to come to us, simply because Smith has disappeared, and because his disappearance is being investigated by us. When they do, we can also talk about what Smith was up to."

"Further to that, I spoke to Patrick Deasy's eldest son this morning, and he's instructed their solicitor and Patrick Deasy's bank to release the information we're looking for about recent financial transactions and sales of assets. It's fortuitous that the car's been found here in Balbriggan, as I was coming here anyway this afternoon to visit the solicitor and the bank."

"Do you think Smith's still alive?" Powers asked, after a pause. "I think you were half expecting to find him in there." He indicated the boot of the car.

"The fact that he hasn't contacted the Embassy isn't a good sign. Doubtless you'll get a better idea of that situation when you speak to the Embassy; but at the moment, I'm inclined to be pessimistic."

At that moment, they were distracted by a slight altercation that was happening a short distance away. A man who was attempting to approach them had been stopped by a Garda officer. Interested, they walked over.

"Martin Edwards, *Balbriggan Enquirer*," the man said as they approached. "Just happened to be passing and saw something was going on. What's the story?"

"No story really," Reilly replied casually. "We're just recovering a car that was reported as stolen. It belongs to a car hire company. It was found intact this morning, and we're in the process of recovering it for routine investigation."

"When was it stolen?"

"It was reported stolen yesterday."

"Where was it stolen?"

"In Dublin."

"Any information about who stole it?"

Reilly shook his head. "The person responsible hasn't been apprehended yet, so we've no information about that at present."

Edwards paused for a moment, looking at the car. "OK, well, if you get any more news about it that you can let me have, give me a call."

He handed a business card to Reilly, who took it somewhat reluctantly. He walked away quickly, stopping once to look back at the car again, before hurrying back to his own car, which was parked near the railway arches. He got in, reached for pen and paper from the glove compartment, and jotted down the number of the stolen hire car, which he had noted and memorised. The car looked remarkably similar to the one he had seen Smith getting into on Drogheda Street a few days earlier. It was definitely the same car hire firm, and the same colour, and probably the same make, although he couldn't be sure of that. He drove straight to Drogheda Street.

Back in his office, he sought out the piece of paper on which he had written down the number of Smith's car. It was the same number as that of the stolen hire car that he had just written down. He stared at the two pieces of paper. It was several days since he had seen Smith getting into the car. This incident might have nothing to do with Smith, who could have returned the car before it was stolen. But what was it doing in Balbriggan if it had been stolen in Dublin? A coincidence? His instinct was to doubt it.

After a moment's thought, he sat down at his computer, logged on, and did a search for the car hire firm. The firm was located at Dublin airport. The firm's website made it clear that the airport was its operating base, where its vehicles were kept. It catered specifically for travellers using the airport, and by implication, those staying at airport hotels. Smith had mentioned the Embassy and might, therefore, have been staying there. But the fact that he had hired a car from this particular firm suggested that he was staying at the airport.

As far as he remembered, there were three hotels at the airport. He did a search, and noted the phone numbers of each hotel. He phoned the first one and asked to speak to Robert Smith, only to be told that there was no one of that name staying at the hotel. With the second hotel, he was in luck.

"Robert Smith?" the receptionist asked.

"Yes. He's an American. I'm not sure of his room number, but I believe he's staying at your hotel. My name's Martin Edwards. I'm from *The Balbriggan Enquirer*."

"Can you hold the line a moment, please?" she asked.

"Yes, OK."

There was a long pause, after which a male voice came on the line.

"Hello, who's speaking, please?"

"My name's Martin Edwards. I'm a senior reporter at *The Balbriggan Enquirer*. I'm speaking from the newspaper offices on Drogheda Street in Balbriggan. Mr Smith paid us a visit here at the newspaper a few days ago, and I was wanting to get some more information on the story he had. Is he available to speak to, or can I leave a message for him to call back?"

"Does he not answer his mobile phone?"

"I'm afraid I don't have his mobile number. I take it that he isn't there at the moment."

There was a short pause.

"Mr Smith has evidently gone missing," the other said. "He hasn't been seen here at the hotel for several days, and didn't check out when he was due to. His hire car has apparently been reported missing by the car hire company. I understand that the Garda are investigating the matter, so you'd probably be best speaking to them."

"I see." It was Edwards' turn to pause. "Who am I speaking to?"

"I'm the hotel manager."

"Right, OK, thank you for that information. If I leave my phone number, could I ask you to call me if you get any news of Mr Smith?"

"Well, I'll take your phone number anyway."

After he had hung up, Edwards sat still for several minutes. If Smith had gone missing, then, at least potentially, he had a big story. The problem was that what he knew was only half a story. What was the financial transaction that Smith had talked about? If agents of the regime had bought one of Patrick Deasy's wagons, why had they done so? What were they intending to do with it? He needed more information. He returned to his car and drove back to the harbour car park. But by the time he got there, the Garda had gone, as had the hire car, which they had presumably taken away.

He parked, and wandered through the railway arches and out onto the quayside. The tide was out, and the boats in the harbour were lying on the muddy expanse of the harbour bottom. There weren't many people about; but he saw that a traffic barrier had been set up across the north quay, about halfway down, and he could see a couple of Garda vehicles some distance beyond it. A number of Garda officers were carrying out some kind of investigation on the quayside near where the vehicles were parked. Edwards wandered over to where an individual was standing watching them. He was wearing a typical fisherman's garb of waterproofs, donkey jacket, and the regulation woolly hat.

Edwards opened the conversation.

"I wonder what's going on over there?"

Woolly Hat was philosophical. "I think it's something to do with the *Maid of Cork*. That's one of the two boats owned by Patrick Deasy until he sold them recently. That's where it normally berths when it's in. There seems to be a lot of interest in that boat all of a sudden."

"By the Garda?"

"By the Garda, presumably, as that's where the boat normally berths. There was also an American down here a few days ago, asking about it. Sharp-cut suit – not the sort you'd have thought would be interested in a fishing boat."

Edwards could hardly believe his luck. "What was his name?"

"Oh, I didn't get his name. But he seemed very interested in who might have bought the boat."

"Do you know who did buy it?"

"Well, there's a thing. As far as I could tell, it was bought by some of our EU friends – Spaniards, maybe. They buy up an Irish boat, and that gives them access to our fishing quota. It's basically a foreign boat flying an Irish flag, so we get that much less of our own quota. It's a trick they've learned. But I heard them talking a couple of times on the quayside, and it certainly wasn't Spanish, or any European language I recognised. And the other day, I caught sight of them through the windows of the deckhouse on their boat. I couldn't make out what they were doing at first; but then I twigged that they were having some kind of prayer meeting – you know, the old Allah routine." He waved his hands in the air.

Edwards stared at him. It was as if the pieces of a jigsaw were all starting to fall into place. A question formed in the back of his mind – the same question that had occurred to Robert Smith.

"A trawler… What the hell would they want with a trawler?"

Liam Powers had hardly sat down at his desk when his phone started ringing. It was Kevin Reilly.

"Right. First of all, it looks as if Smith was on to something. Among Patrick Deasy's asset sales was the disposal of two fishing boats he owned in Balbriggan harbour. One of the boats was sold to a French national of Middle Eastern origin – someone called Iqbal Mohammed. The boat is apparently now crewed by French nationals who are all of Middle Eastern origin. Secondly, I've just received a report from Forensics about the DNA swabs we took at the place where Patrick Deasy fell. Two of the swabs are definitely from an individual with a Middle Eastern genetic background. This means that the investigation into Patrick Deasy's death has now become a murder investigation."

"Middle Eastern origin – which country?" asked Powers.

"I'll give you three guesses."

10

It was the slightest creak of a floorboard on the landing outside the room that gave Miriam forewarning of the attack. Even so, she only had time to turn and duck down behind a chair before the door burst open and the intruder was in the room.

The light in the room was dim, as the curtains were drawn, so it was two or three seconds before the intruder, who was carrying a pistol, located Miriam. Before he had swung the pistol round, she had time to seize an un-drunk cup of tea on the table and dash the contents into his face. The shot he fired missed, and before he recovered, she had kicked him as hard as she could in the crotch, causing him to double over in agony.

She didn't wait, but dashed out of the door, down the stairs and outside into the street. She knew she was running for her life, and that her life probably depended on the fact that she still had her car keys in her pocket. Her handbag, with her phone, cards and other documents, was still in her room. It would have been suicidal to have waited even a second to try and grab them. The only consolation was that her phone was switched off, and that the electronic security was unbreakable.

Once in her car, Miriam gunned the engine of the big Toyota and raced down the street. She knew that this was going to be the drive of her life, because she was driving for her life. She was going north, making for the border. Her main disadvantage was that, now that she had evidently been discovered, it would be obvious to her pursuer where she would be headed.

She joined the main boulevard running around the northern side of the city, keeping to the outside lane. The traffic was fairly light, so she was able to keep her speed up. At one point, she passed a police car, going the other way. She eyed it warily, but it drove past without any response. Either her assailant had not yet notified the police about her, or he was operating on his own. In view of the nature of the information she had, the latter was probably more likely. The security surrounding the project had been absolutely watertight – or almost…

She turned off the boulevard into the exit for the road which ran north out of the city. This was a smaller, single-track road, but still with a tarmac surface, and quite good for this country. Soon, the road was running out into the desert: settlements and houses became sparse, and eventually the landscape was empty of human habitation. Ahead, the land rose into a range of barren, dun-coloured hills, which seemed to bar her way to the north. The road began to climb and turn as it reached the hills. There was no signposting here, so the car's satnav was now crucial in making sure she didn't lose her way. There was a good hour's drive ahead of her. It would be the most critical hour of her life.

As the road climbed, the mountains closed in around her; but it was possible to see further where the mountains didn't obstruct her view. She was keeping a watchful eye on the road behind her through the mirror. There was very little traffic: she passed a truck going the other way, and overtook an old tractor, but for a while saw nothing else. From time to time she also cast glances at the sky for any sign of search aircraft. If her pursuer had contacted the authorities, sending a search aircraft up to look for her would be the obvious thing to do. But she saw no sign of any aircraft. This puzzled her. If her pursuer hadn't notified the authorities, what was he up to? He might have taken a short while to recover from the kick she had given him; but only a short while, if that. If he wanted to catch her, he wouldn't waste time searching her room or trying to break into her phone – others could do that.

At length, she got her answer. Looking in the mirror, she thought she caught a glimpse of something on the road behind her. Because the road was twisting and turning all the time, it was a couple of minutes before she confirmed that there was definitely another vehicle on the road behind her. It was some distance away, but she hadn't seen it in previous glances in the mirror, so that indicated that it must gradually be overhauling her. Instinctively, she pressed down on the accelerator, although she was already driving about as fast as possible on this road.

As the minutes passed, it became clear that the other vehicle was gaining on her. It seemed to be quite small, and repeated glances in the mirror revealed it to be some kind of sports car. It would therefore be faster than her vehicle, and, being small and low-slung, would have better road-holding capability, enabling it to take corners faster than she could. Although she could not see who was driving the other car, she had no doubt that it was her pursuer. She could remember his face, even though she only saw it for a few seconds. She would never forget it.

As her pursuer closed the distance between them, she had to decide what she was going to do. If she allowed him to get right behind her, he would then be close enough to start shooting. He might even try to pull alongside her, although that would be very risky on this road. She looked at the satnav. About a kilometre ahead, a small track left the road on the right. It rejoined the road some distance further north, not far from the border. In terms of distance, it was a short-cut. However, in terms of time, it almost certainly wouldn't be. If it was anything like the mountain tracks in this country that she knew about, progress on it would be slow, even in a four-wheel-drive vehicle. But while the big Toyota would be able to cope with even a rough mountain track, she doubted whether her pursuer's low-slung sports car would be able to at almost any speed. It was her only option.

As the turn-off to the track approached, she kept her speed up, braking at the last second, and half-skidding onto the track. By this time, her pursuer was only about a hundred metres or so behind her. Even so, she slowed down as much as she dared. The further she was able to draw her pursuer along the track, the greater would be her advantage. Looking in the mirror, she saw that her pursuer had followed her onto the track. Because she had slowed, he had closed the distance between them some more. He was now almost within shooting distance. She gradually increased her speed, opening the distance out to about a hundred metres again. At that speed, he was still able to keep up with her. She didn't want to discourage him too soon.

He was evidently doing his best to try and close the distance, but at the speed they were going, the sports car was visibly bouncing on the rough stony track, its wheels sometimes leaving the ground. The sports car's suspension wasn't going to be able to take much more of that kind of treatment. She allowed the distance to close slightly, and managed to continue thus for another three kilometres.

She then reached a turn where the track started to climb steeply as it traversed the side of a mountain. As it did so, the track became a lot rougher, without even the pretence of surfacing that had characterised it thus far. The ill-defined wheel tracks now ran over massive cobbles and potholes. The suspension started to protest, and she had to drop a gear and slow right down. At a much-reduced speed, the big Toyota proved more than capable of coping with even this mountain track.

But the drop in speed meant that her pursuer was quickly able to catch up with her. She heard a shot; then another. Something struck the Toyota at the back somewhere: she was under fire. She increased her speed as much as she dared. The suspension protested, but there were no further shots. Glancing in her mirror, she saw why. Her pursuer's car had come to a halt, slewed across the road. It had been unable to negotiate more than a few metres of the rougher track after the turn. Even if its suspension hadn't gone, the low-slung chassis would be grounding over the massive potholes. It was simply not built for that kind of terrain.

As she pulled away from him, she knew his only option would be to see if he could get back to the road and try to intercept her on the road further north. In her last glimpse of him in her mirror, he was evidently trying to reverse out of a pothole in order to make his way back down the track.

Everything now depended on her being able to reach the point where the track rejoined the road before her pursuer did. Even in the Toyota, the going would be slow. It wasn't just a matter of how much punishment the vehicle would take, but also of simply staying on the track as it wound above precipitous drops along the side of the mountain.

An ordinary driver could not have done it. But Miriam was no ordinary driver. During her service with the IDF, she had taken advanced driver training in the Negev with some of the best instructors in the world. There were few drivers who could now match Miriam's ability to drive in this kind of terrain. She now pushed the big Toyota to its limit, sometimes skidding perilously close to the edge of precipices as the track wound through the mountains. At length, the track began to descend again. As it did so, its surface improved, and as the terrain began to level out, she was able to pick up some speed.

As she approached the end of the track, she slowed slightly to give herself time to scan the junction for any sign of her pursuer. The terrain was now flat enough for her to see the junction and the road clearly from some distance away. There was no sign of her pursuer in the vicinity of the junction, so she accelerated onto the road. Once back on the tarmac, she was able to increase speed still further, although the road still twisted and turned as it wound along the floor of a shallow valley.

There was no sign of any problem ahead, but she noticed smoke somewhere on the road behind her. The source of the smoke appeared to be moving. A minute later, this was explained when a vehicle hove into view behind her. It was her pursuer. Smoke was billowing back from his car, which was evidently on fire somewhere. More than likely the suspension had collapsed, and the tyres were scoring against the chassis, and the rubber was burning off. There was a lot of smoke: huge clouds of it.

Her pursuer was literally flogging his car to death in his attempt to catch her. And he was succeeding. Despite the fact that Miriam had increased her speed by as much as the road allowed, he was still gaining on her. At that rate, he would catch up with her in just over a minute. But the border was now less than two kilometres away.

She reached the top of a rise, and this brought the border posts into view in the distance. She raced for the line, but before she reached it, her pursuer caught up with her. He opened fire: bullets began hitting the Toyota. She crouched down in her seat and started to weave to spoil his aim. As she approached the border post, she suddenly slammed on her brakes. Her pursuer did not have time to react, and his car rammed into the back of the Toyota, bringing it to a stop. Before the astonished border guards had time to react, Miriam accelerated away again towards the line.

But her pursuer was still not deterred. Somehow, he managed to get the wrecked car going again. As Miriam crossed the border, he pulled alongside her, and began shooting into the side of the Toyota. She was crouching down in her seat, now driving blind. A bullet struck her hand on the steering wheel; another tore through the back of the seat behind her. She twisted the steering wheel, weaving violently to spoil his aim. But she lost control, and the car turned over, rolling several times before coming to rest on its side.

As the car rolled, she was shaken about like a rag doll, and crushed against the steering wheel. She felt several of her ribs break. As the car came to rest, she lay dazed, unable to move. There was pain in her chest, and there was something wrong with her leg, which was trapped under the dashboard. Her pursuer got out of his car and walked over to the Toyota, pistol in hand, to finish her off.

In his intent, he had not noticed that the border guards on this side, where he now was, having recovered from their surprise, had run towards the crashed Toyota. One of them called out a warning, but he took no notice. He raised his pistol and aimed at Miriam through the cracked windscreen as she lay trapped in the driver's seat.

But the border guard, having levelled his sub-machine gun, briefly squeezed the trigger. Miriam's pursuer took the burst full in the chest. It bowled him over, and he ended up sprawled in the dust. The guard walked over to the man, but it was immediately obvious that he was dead.

He turned his attention to the Toyota. Miriam was conscious, and gritting her teeth against the pain in her chest, hand and leg. The guard tapped out the remains of the windscreen with the butt of his gun, and leaned in to speak to her. She nodded in response, but for the moment was unable to speak. Another guard was already on his mobile phone. The guard continued to talk to Miriam, although she still couldn't say much in reply. A third guard looked speculatively at the Toyota, weighing up the possibility of pulling it upright again. He decided to leave it until assistance arrived.

The air ambulance helicopter was the first to arrive, setting down in a cloud of dust a short distance from the Toyota. A doctor and two paramedics emerged and walked over to the car. There was a short conversation in which the border guards explained briefly what had happened. The doctor leaned in through the gap where the windscreen had been, and made an initial assessment of Miriam's condition. By now she could respond briefly to questions, although it was clear that she was in considerable pain.

The doctor established that she had several broken or fractured bones, as well as a bullet injury to the hand, which meant that she would have to be anaesthetised before they could attempt to lift her out of the car. There was no obvious sign of serious head injury, but she would need X-rays and scans of her head as soon as possible on reaching hospital. If it wasn't possible to pull the car upright, they would have to lift her out of the car through the windscreen, which would be difficult.

At that point, however, three police cars arrived from the nearby town. After assessing the situation, one of the cars was positioned with its back end facing the roof of the Toyota. A rope was tied round the door pillar of the Toyota and run round the towbar on the back of the police car. Two policemen gently pushed the Toyota over as the other policemen and the border guards took the strain on the other end of the rope, and slowly lowered the car back onto its wheels. Although the car was battered, the front doors still opened, and two policemen worked quickly to unbolt the driver's seat from its rails.

By this time, Miriam was becoming more vocal. She had experienced some pain when the car was lowered onto its wheels, but now another concern filled her mind. As the doctor started to speak to her, she interrupted him.

"I must speak to the Ambassador," she said. "Please, it's important – I must speak to the Ambassador."

But the doctor had his own priorities, which he was clear about. "All in good time. We need to get you to hospital as soon as possible to check for serious head injury. I can't see any signs of it, but it's essential we do checks as soon as possible."

"But I must speak to the Ambassador as soon as possible. It's a matter of vital importance."

But the doctor was insistent. "You will speak to the Ambassador as soon as possible after we get you to hospital. But we can do nothing until we can get you out of this car. Because you have broken bones, it's essential to anaesthetise you before we do that, so I'm going to give you an injection now."

"But…"

He wagged his finger at her. "You are under my care, and I will have no arguments."

She realised the futility of further argument, and nodded in resignation. A needle slid into her arm, and a minute later, she slid into unconsciousness. Two policemen lifted the seat, with Miriam in it, out of the car, and set it down on the ground beside the stretcher from the helicopter. The paramedics took over, and carefully transferred Miriam to the stretcher. A few minutes later, Miriam was airborne, as the helicopter flew back to the hospital.

When she awoke again, it would be too late for the information she had to be of any use, as it would be out of date. Thus, her pursuer achieved his objective in the end, albeit in a way he had not intended. Because he had not delayed even for a minute in his pursuit of Miriam, he had not advised his superiors of the situation. Had he done so, they would have passed the information on, and that would almost certainly have resulted in the mission being cancelled. But because those in charge of the mission remained in ignorance of the fact that there had been a breach of their security, Musa Khalid gave the fateful order for the mission to proceed.

11

The mud at the bottom of the harbour proved to be deeper than Robert Smith had anticipated. Having climbed down the ladder attached to the harbour wall, he stepped cautiously off the bottom rung, to find that the Wellington boots he was wearing sank nearly a foot into the mud. He had to grip the boots with his feet to hang onto them each time he raised a foot to take a step. Pulling the boots out of the mud made a glutinous sucking noise, which meant that he had to be even more cautious with each step he took.

His progress was therefore slow, and to reach his objective, he had to negotiate his way around the hulls of several boats lying on the harbour bottom. His objective was the fishing boat *Maid of Cork*, which, not having left on the evening high tide, would therefore be in harbour overnight. He had spent much of the evening sitting in his car in the harbour-side car park. He had parked in a space where he had a clear view of the *Maid of Cork* in the harbour, through the railway arches. He had not seen any sign of activity on the boat, so he was assuming that it was currently unoccupied. This would be the first opportunity he had had to get close enough to the boat to examine it without being seen: at night, at low tide, with the boat in harbour.

However, first he had to reach it. The *Maid of Cork* was some distance along the harbour wall from where the ladder was, and floundering around in the mud of the harbour bottom was far from pleasant. There was enough light from the quayside for him to see the various boats lying on the harbour bottom, but not always smaller obstructions. A couple of times he nearly fell when he tripped over mooring ropes that were all but invisible in the dark. Floundering about in such a way meant that it was difficult to avoid making quite a lot of noise. As he approached the *Maid of Cork*, therefore, he stopped and stood still for two or three minutes, looking and listening for any signs of life on board the boat. But there were none; the boat was in darkness.

As quietly as he could, he made his way over to the boat. He approached the stern of the boat. Before doing anything else, he wanted to examine the boat's propeller. Earlier in the day, he had driven his car onto the quayside on the other side of the harbour from where the *Maid of Cork* was moored, and surreptitiously scrutinised the boat through a pair of binoculars. One of the things he had noticed was that there was something distinctly odd about its propeller, although even with binoculars he hadn't been able to make out exactly what it was. The propeller was well under the stern of the boat, so he had to steady himself with his left hand against the boat's hull and lean forward until he could look under the hull and shine his torch onto the propeller.

There was a single propeller with three blades, one of which was partly buried in the mud. It was a standard boat propeller, but attached to each blade, or those he could see, was a piece of plastic. Another piece of plastic was attached to the end of the keel in such a way that it would come into contact with the pieces of plastic attached to the propeller blades when the propeller turned. The pieces of plastic were not uniform, and rather irregularly shaped – the whole thing was clearly some kind of lash-up. He was puzzled as to its purpose, although it would certainly make a lot of noise underwater when the vessel was under way. He took a picture of it with his phone, then stood upright again.

He turned his attention to the business of climbing up on board the boat. The stern was the lowest part of the hull, and there was a mooring rope attached to it, which trailed down into the mud from its attachment on the quayside before reaching the boat. He shone his torch along it, judging how he could use it to climb on board.

As he was looking at the rope, he failed to see a figure move forward on the darkened deck of the boat, above and behind him. Silently, the figure raised its arm. A heavy blow struck Robert Smith on the back of the head, and he pitched forward face down into the mud.

12

As Liam Powers had predicted, it was the Americans who were eventually obliged to make the journey from their Embassy on Elgin Road to the rather anonymous-looking building on Harcourt Street where he had his office. Kevin Reilly was already there when the visitors were ushered into Powers' office. They introduced themselves as a Mr Garcia, Second Secretary for Cultural Affairs at the Embassy, and his assistant, a Mr Rogan. In fact, Sandor Rogan was nothing of the kind; but he had assumed the role for the purposes of this interview. Privately, Reilly doubted whether either of them had much to do with cultural affairs.

Liam Powers opened the conversation. "Thank you for coming over, gentlemen. You've come to talk to us about Robert Smith."

It was a statement rather than a question. The Americans indicated that they had.

Powers continued. "The facts we're working with are, first of all, that Robert Smith, who arrived in this country nine days ago, has disappeared. He didn't check out of his hotel when he was due to, two days ago, and hasn't been seen there for several days. He didn't return the hire car he had, when it was due for return, also two days ago. The car has since been located. It was found, apparently abandoned, in a car park near the harbour in Balbriggan, a small town a few miles north of Dublin. It's been temporarily impounded, pending the conclusion of our investigations into this matter. Apart from the car, we currently have no trace of Mr Smith, or his whereabouts. Can you shed any light on where Mr Smith might be?"

"I'm afraid we don't know where Mr Smith is, no," said Michael Garcia. "Obviously we're very concerned if one of our citizens has gone missing. We were hoping that you might have some information about him."

"We're pursuing lines of inquiry in relation to the matter, some of which have produced possible leads," said Reilly. "Do you have any information about what Mr Smith was doing in Balbriggan?"

"I'm afraid I don't, no," said Michael Garcia. His assistant remained silent.

"So it would come as a surprise to you to learn that Mr Smith had been making enquiries about a local businessman in Balbriggan, Patrick Deasy?" continued Reilly.

"Patrick Deasy... Indeed?"

"And that Patrick Deasy died twelve days ago, in suspicious circumstances – a death which is now the subject of a murder investigation?"

"I didn't know that, no," said Michael Garcia. He was starting to look uncomfortable.

"Do you know what Mr Smith's particular interest in Patrick Deasy was?"

"Well... er... I'm not sure I'm able to say..."

"So you weren't aware that Mr Smith was investigating a financial transaction that was alleged to have taken place between Patrick Deasy and representatives of the regime that you refer to as The Adversaries?"

The two Americans looked at each other, in manifest consternation.

"Where… did you get that from?" asked Sandor Rogan, after he had recovered from his surprise.

Kevin Reilly answered him. "I interviewed Robert Smith after he turned up at the office of Patrick Deasy's firm in Balbriggan, evidently not being aware that Patrick Deasy was dead. Smith told me what at the time I considered to be a cock and bull story about a financial transaction by Patrick Deasy involving agents of the regime you refer to as The Adversaries. Events since then mean that we've had to reassess the validity of Smith's story."

"He… should not have divulged such information," said Sandor Rogan. "It was highly classified."

"Well, we're hardly going to place an announcement about it in *The Irish Times*," Reilly commented dryly. "In any event, it's now become part of the investigation into Patrick Deasy's death. In fact, it's one of the reasons why that has now become a murder investigation."

"Why is that?"

"First of all, we now have information that among Patrick Deasy's recent financial transactions was the sale of a fishing boat he owned at Balbriggan to a French national of Middle Eastern origin, called Iqbal Mohammed," Reilly continued. "The boat is now crewed by French nationals, all of Middle Eastern origin. Secondly, DNA swabs taken at the scene of Patrick Deasy's death include traces of DNA from an individual with a Middle Eastern genetic background. These two facts mean that we can no longer regard Patrick Deasy's death as an accident or suicide. We're now treating it as murder."

"Iqbal Mohammed is known to us," said Sandor Rogan. "That confirms the link with The Adversaries. Have you apprehended the crew of the boat?"

"No, not yet. We only received this information earlier today. As soon as we received it, we sent officers to Balbriggan to apprehend the crew; but the boat had apparently sailed on this afternoon's high tide. We've put out an alert to the Garda nationally, that they're to be apprehended if they put into any Irish port. We've also made a similar request to the UK and France, in case they turn up there."

"So you don't know where the boat is now?"

"It's presumably somewhere out in the Irish Sea."

13

At 1.15 am, Constable Damien Brown of the Sellafield site police set off on the routine night patrol along his section of the southern perimeter fence. It was June, and although the sky was cloudy, obscuring the stars, there was no rain, and the light westerly breeze was mild, almost warm. It was an ordinary night, with no unusual alerts, and Constable Brown wasn't expecting any trouble. If there was any trouble, it was rather to be found within the site than outside it. The main site was in the middle of a major programme of downsizing, as the operating companies shed labour to cut costs. There had been some unrest, with a series of strikes and other industrial action, and the general level of morale among the workforce was low.

The downsizing was continuing despite the massive construction project on the new site to the north-west of the main site. The new build, for one of the new generation of nuclear power stations, was being undertaken by a consortium led by a Pakistani firm, the Pakistan Nuclear Company, which had won the contract with the backing of Saudi money. Much of the contract labour building the power station was from Pakistan or the Gulf, and although some of the general workforce operating the power station would be local, the PNC wanted to bring in many of its own people from Pakistan. As the new reactors were a PNC design, all the engineers and technical staff would be from Pakistan. A large new mosque was being built in Whitehaven, and another was planned to be built in Seascale for the technical and managerial staff.

All this meant that there were few opportunities at the new site for those being made redundant on the main site, and none at all for engineers and technical staff – hence the low morale. The large influx of foreigners into the area had caused potentially serious security problems for the site; but the site police and security had been told that anyone working for the PNC consortium was to be given whatever access they required, with no questions asked. The head of security had simply shrugged in resignation. If that was what the big chiefs wanted, then they would be responsible for any consequences. It was said that the Pakistanis and the Saudis were hoping to be able to tap into leaks of nuclear information at Sellafield. Everything leaked these days, especially at Sellafield.

Constable Brown came to the end of his beat, stopped, and switched on his flashlight briefly. After a minute, he was joined by Constable Wilson, who had reached the end of his beat from the opposite direction. They exchanged greetings and stood chatting for a couple of minutes. The conversation turned inevitably to the latest issues at work.

"Any sign of the guard strike being called off?" asked Keith Wilson. A private guard service shared the security role with the site police – mostly manning the gates and checking vehicles going in and out – but they were much less well paid.

"No, it's still definitely on. The firm's management has confirmed that Charlie Graham isn't going to be reinstated, and because the complaint against him was made by one of our Asian friends, no appeal will be allowed; so the strike's continuing."

"The whole thing sounds like a complete cock-up to me. You wonder where things are going next."

"I've heard that the management plans to break the strike by subcontracting to another security firm."

"If they can rely on their employees to break the strike."

"Well, the strike's pretty solid at the moment, so there's not a lot else they can do."

"It'll still take a while to get security clearance for another firm. That'll mean no chance of leave for the foreseeable future."

"Be good for overtime, though."

"Aye, if that's what you want. I'd rather spend time with the family. I can't wait until my retirement: I'm counting the days. I've more than had enough of this place. I'm old enough to remember when this place was the future. Things were bright and optimistic. You could think that things were going to get better in the future. Now it's just a cesspit crawling with foreigners."

"Well, it certainly looks as if things are going to get worse before they get better. I won't deny that I envy you being so close to retirement. I don't have any confidence that I've got a job here for life."

"The people who run this place aren't fit to run a whelk stall, let alone a nuclear establishment. If there's a wrong way of doing something, you can guarantee that they'll find it. You'd think that the new power station would put this place back on track, but that's turning out to be a massive cock-up as well. It makes me despair for the future."

"Well, at least it looks like it's going to be a quiet night. Should be an easy coast home to the end of the shift. Will you be at the rugby on Saturday?"

"Aye, my son'll be playing, so I'll be along to watch."

"I'll maybe see you there, then."

Each man began to retrace his steps back to his respective guard post. Some distance away, a vixen began giving an alarm call, repeated again and again into the night.

A mile out to sea, Ahmed brought the *Maid of Cork* round in a wide turn, completing a circle as he throttled the engine back to idling speed. He was concerned about the schedule, as they were two minutes late for the arrival time. The *Maid of Cork* drifted to a stop in the water, rocking only slightly, as there was very little swell and hardly any breeze. Ahmed blipped the engine four times, waiting five seconds between each blip.

A hundred metres away, the surface of the sea began to foam and churn. A conning tower, surmounted by two periscopes, emerged from the water, followed by the rest of the submarine as the sea cascaded from the long dark hull. Even before the water had finished draining from the hull, the deck hatches clanged open, and men in matt black helmets and combat uniforms scrambled out.

Long containers were lifted out of the deck hatches and opened up on deck. Each contained a black rubber inflatable commando boat. The boats were inflated and assembled, then dropped down into the water alongside.

More containers and equipment were lifted out of the hatches – racks of weapons, including a 20 mm gun, two heavy machine guns and a mortar; ammunition boxes; containers for specialist equipment; backpacks. Most of these were loaded into the boats alongside by some of the submarine's crew, while the soldiers strapped on weapons and equipment.

The soldiers formed up in groups, each group allocated to one of the boats, and began to board the boats in turn. When each boat was ready, it moved away from the submarine and took up station a few metres away, waiting to depart. Meanwhile, Ahmed had positioned the *Maid of Cork* astern of the submarine, with the boat's stern facing the shore, to screen the submarine from radar surveillance from the south. Neither the *Maid of Cork* nor the submarine was showing any lights. Ahmed had been passed a pair of night-vision goggles from one of the boats, and was now using these to enable him to keep the *Maid of Cork* in position, with the engine idling. The boats were assembling on the far side of the submarine from the shore, so that the use of small torches in the boats while loading them would not be visible from the shore.

The first boats away carried the assault group whose initial task was to secure the beachhead. They curved round the bow of the submarine and headed for the shore. In the dark, they were invisible almost immediately, and the noise from their muffled engines became inaudible by the time they were 100 metres away.

Even from a mile away, the lights of Sellafield extended along quite a length of the coast ahead. It was the size of a small town. As they approached the coast, many of the lights dropped below the line of sight, and the shoreline darkened; but key personnel in each boat were wearing night-vision goggles, and for them at least, their objective remained clearly in view. Their objective was the bridge which carried the waste discharge pipes across the river and down to the ground.

As the boats approached the beach, they took up formation in line abreast, about ten metres apart. There was hardly any surf, and in the last few metres, the engines were cut and tilted out of the water. The lead soldiers in each boat scrambled out over the bows and hauled each boat up onto the beach. The beach was deserted – there was no sign of any opposition.

Once on the beach, the soldiers formed up into their assault groups, each led by a Sergeant, and immediately moved off to take their objectives. The compound around the place where the waste discharge pipes reached the ground was secured, and pickets set north and south of it. Screens were held up to hide any sparks, while diamond-tipped cutters sliced through the security fence around the compound like a hot knife through butter, and within seconds, a large piece of the fence had been taken out. The compound was quickly checked before the leading assault group climbed onto the bridge and, keeping low, cautiously made their way across. Once on the embankment on the far side, they established a temporary defensive position on the top of a low mound, then signalled back across the river with infra-red signal lamps that the first objective had been taken.

By this time, the rest of the boats were approaching the beach. They were given clearance to land, and once beached, the main force scrambled ashore and unloaded the rest of the equipment for the assault. Reinforcements crossed the bridge and set up the 20 mm gun in the defensive position on top of the mound. From this point, there was a commanding view all around – in particular, the gun could be brought to bear on the railway both north and south of the bridge, as well as on the main access road from the north.

Within ten minutes, all the equipment required had been brought over the bridge. The main assault group assembled near the southern end of the long strip containing the conduit for the waste discharge pipes. The strip was still enclosed by its own fence, even though the whole of it was now within the Sellafield site outer boundary, as the land to the north and south of it was now also part of the site. Immediately to the north of the strip was the B1600 complex, containing the Small Research Reactor, which was their objective. The B1600 complex was surrounded by its own security fence, on concrete posts topped with razor wire, which meant that there was a double fence along its boundary with the strip.

For a minute, everything was still while the officer commanding the assault, Major Yusuf Khan, surveyed the situation from the defensive position on top of the mound. He scrutinised the guard post at the old Main Gate, 200 metres away. The gate was not currently in use, as the access road to it had been temporarily closed during the construction of the new build; but the guard post was evidently still in use, as Major Khan confirmed, looking at it through binoculars.

Constable Keith Wilson, visible through the windows

of the guard hut, was unaware that he was being observed. The assault force was on the far side of the mound on which the defensive post had been set up, and was therefore out of sight. The mound also blocked the view from the guard post of their objective, the Small Research Reactor within the B1600 complex.

Beyond the guard post, Khan could see a man wearing a high-visibility jacket walking between two buildings in the distance; but apart from that, there was no sign of activity. The other guard post visible was further away – some 400 metres to the south. The mound blocked the view from that guard post also, as did a large shed just to the north of the guard post.

He turned his attention to the B1600 complex. The complex was well lit, and from his vantage point on top of the mound, he had an excellent view of it. Its location and layout might almost have been designed to facilitate an operation of this kind. The largest building in the complex, B1602, containing the Small Research Reactor, was immediately in front of him. It was also the building nearest the boundary fence of the complex facing the sea. The building was L-shaped, with the base of the L on the far side, as he was looking at it, pointing inland. According to the map he had, based on one supplied by Alan Southam, the reactor was located at the corner of the L. A tall chimney stack protruded into the night from somewhere behind it. The radioactive store attached to the reactor was at the other end of the base of the L.

Alongside B1602, and parallel with it, were two long, narrow buildings, B1600 and B1601 according to the map. B1601, alongside B1602, mostly contained auxiliary support systems for the reactor, while B1600 mostly contained laboratories and offices. The main car park was next to the entrance to the complex from the access road. Around and between the buildings, the ground was covered by an expanse of smooth concrete.

There was no sign of any activity within the complex. The only sounds audible at that moment were from a short distance away on the western side of the mound, where soldiers with spades were filling sacks with earth dug out of the side of the mound. Major Khan glanced at his watch. They were back on schedule, having made good time during the landing operation. He took another careful look round through the binoculars, then looked at his watch again, this time with some concern. They were now a minute behind schedule.

Then the phone in his top pocket beeped to indicate a text message. He looked at it – it was just one word: "Ready."

He was about to give the order to move, when his attention was caught by a car approaching along the access road. It turned into the car park for the B1600 complex, and parked. A man got out, walked over to the security gate into the complex and let himself in. He walked over to building B1600, and disappeared behind it; but he was obviously making for the entrance on the far side of the building, which was indicated on Khan's map. A minute later, a light went on in a window on the near side of the building. Major Khan leaned over to speak to Sergeant Tariq Abdullah on his right.

"The man who just went into that building…"

Sergeant Abdullah nodded.

"If he appears again during the operation, particularly if he moves towards the reactor building, take him out. Single shot if you can."

Again, Sergeant Abdullah nodded. "I can get him with one shot, sir."

There was no time for further delay. On Major Khan's signal, the first assault group moved forward. The diamond-tipped cutters sliced through the first fence, surrounding the conduit, creating a gate that was pulled open inwards. Seconds later, a second gate was cut into the fence around the B1600 complex. First through was a soldier carrying a large polythene bag and a long stick. He moved along the fence for a short distance before crossing over to the end wall of B1602, where a CCTV camera was fixed, looking along the length of the wall. Using the stick, he placed the bag over the camera. The thick polythene allowed light through, but prevented the camera from focusing an image. Next were the explosives team, closely followed by several soldiers dragging the earth-filled sacks behind them. The main entrance to B1602 was on the long side of the building facing away from the sea, near its southern end. The south end of the building, facing the mound, was blank, with no windows or doors.

Once against the end wall, the soldiers were hidden from view from any distance, and could effectively work unobserved. The explosives team identified the location on the wall for the charges, using a diagram based on information supplied by Alan Southam. Lengths of detonating cord were fixed to the wall: to these were attached electric detonators and fuse. They were then covered by the sacks of earth to concentrate the blast and muffle the sound of the explosion. The fuse was trailed around the corner to the seaward side of the building, where they all assembled.

The muffled thud of the explosion briefly disturbed the night – the sacks of earth proved quite effective in masking the noise, which was masked further by the mound. Two hundred metres away, Keith Wilson looked up from his desk. He had heard a muffled thud from somewhere to the north. But large-scale construction work on the new build site was now going on day and night, and such noises were heard from time to time, especially at night. He listened for another minute, but heard nothing further, and concluded that it must have been from the construction work.

Seconds after the explosion, the main assault group was through the fences. After clearing away the debris, they climbed through the gap in the wall created by the explosion, led by Lieutenant Mohamed Qasim. The main hall of B1602 was deserted as the soldiers climbed through. According to the information supplied by Alan Southam, most of the night shift would be having their mid-shift break in the rest room at that moment. On the left-hand side of the main hall was a series of equipment and storage bays, leading down to the reactor at the far end. On the right-hand side were changing rooms, toilets and showers, and various offices. The rest room was round the corner in the base of the L of the building, opposite the main equipment bay. On one side of the equipment bay was the reactor control room; on the other was the radioactive store.

Lieutenant Qasim advanced down the main hall with the lead soldiers, while more soldiers climbed through the gap and followed down the hall. A Sergeant Technician removed an inspection panel near the door, identified the phone line into the building, and disconnected it.

As Lieutenant Qasim approached the far end of the main hall, a man walked round the corner into the main hall and started walking towards them. After a few steps, however, he stopped, obviously uncertain of who they were or what to do. As they came up to him, Lieutenant Qasim spoke to the man in English and told him to put his hands up and face the wall. The man did as he was told, and a soldier frisked him for weapons or phones.

Qasim held his hand up to prevent the soldiers advancing further. He then walked round the corner on his own. In front of him, a corridor led to the end of the base of the L of the building, where there was a security door. On the left-hand side of the corridor was the main equipment bay and the side of the radioactive store. On the right hand side was a series of doors leading to various rooms and offices, and at the far end, male and female toilets. He could hear sounds from the other side of the door immediately to his right, which opened onto the main rest room, where the night shift were nearing the end of their mid-shift break. He looked at the soldier guarding their prisoner.

"Bring him over here," he said. He then motioned the other soldiers to follow. As they did so, he screwed a silencer onto the barrel of his sub-machine gun.

"When I open the door, shove him through," he said to the soldier guarding the prisoner. He grasped the door handle and flung the door open. The soldier then pushed the hapless Dave Turner forward, planted a boot in the small of his back and sent him sprawling into the room.

The buzz of conversation in the room was silenced in sudden astonishment. Lieutenant Qasim stepped forward into the doorway.

"Now hear this," he said, speaking in English. "This building is now temporarily under our control. You will all remain in this room until you are told you can leave. We will shoot anyone who attempts to leave before then. We will be guarding this door. If any of you attempt to raise the alarm, or if British security forces arrive whilst we are still here, then whatever else happens, you are all dead. We will make sure of that."

He raised his sub-machine gun and fired two quick bursts into the air, shooting out several of the lights in the ceiling towards the far end of the room. Because of the silencer, the gun only made a muffled popping noise, but the sound of bullets ripping up the ceiling, and the glass and debris that showered down on those at that end of the room made the point well enough. He stepped back and slammed the door shut. A steel wire was slipped around the door handle, run along the wall and secured to the handle of the next door along the corridor, preventing the door from being opened from the inside. Being an internal room, the rest room didn't have a window.

Inside the room, the stunned silence continued for several seconds.

Eventually, it was Martin Little who broke the silence. "Who the fucking hell are they?"

The question was addressed to Dave Turner, who, having picked himself up from the floor and sat down on a chair, was ruefully rubbing his elbow, which had been bruised when he fell. He shook his head.

"God knows. I don't know. Foreign soldiers of some sort. I went out just now because I heard some sort of bang from outside. When I went round the corner into the main hall, there they were – a whole group of them. They're all dressed the same – black uniforms and helmets, and all carrying machine guns. I saw that they've blown a hole in the wall at the far end. That must've been the bang I heard, and that's how they must've got in without any alarms going off. They all pointed their guns at me, then that guy who spoke told me to put my hands up. I was frisked, then marched round and shoved in here."

"But who are they?" asked Shona Graham. "Where the hell've they come from?"

Dave Turner shrugged. "They look like soldiers to me. Like regular soldiers, with all the combat kit on. When I was outside just now, I heard them talking to each other, and it wasn't any language I recognised – not French or German or owt like that. So, God knows who they are."

"What the fuck are we going to do?" asked Martin Little. "We should let someone know. Has anyone got a phone on them?"

But no one had. Breaking the rule about mobile phones could lead to instant dismissal, and in the current situation, no one was prepared to take the risk. They had all left their mobile phones in their cars. It was only Alan Southam who had no longer felt constrained by the threat – but no one had thought of that.

Kevin Johnston, one of the process workers, casually picked up the receiver of the landline phone in the rest room. He put it to his ear, then put it down again.

"It's dead," he announced. "They've maybe cut the phone line."

"That guy said they'd kill us if the security people turn up whilst they're here," said Dave Turner. "That means that we're hostages. I think we should barricade the door to try and keep them out, and at least give ourselves a chance."

Everyone agreed with that, and so as quietly as possible, they began to move tables and chairs and pile them across the doorway.

Outside, Lieutenant Qasim walked through the entrance to the main equipment bay, to find Alan Southam waiting for them.

"You are Alan Southam?" Qasim asked in English. He had been shown a photograph of Southam, but just wanted to make sure.

Southam nodded. "You're late," he said.

"There was a slight delay before we could move forward into here, but it's not a problem. Is everything ready?"

"Everything's ready. The radioactive store is open, and all the irradiated sheets are now in carrier frames, as are the replacement sheets of enriched uranium. It's up to you now."

"Good."

A soldier came into the bay. "The building's been checked, sir, and there are no more British unaccounted for."

Qasim nodded, then walked back into the corridor and gave the signal for the operation to commence. Two Sergeant Technicians, followed by several soldiers, went into the radioactive store. The Sergeant Technicians checked the store over first with Geiger counters, then turned their attention to the carrier frames, checking each one carefully with the Geiger counters. After each carrier was checked, it was picked up by a soldier wearing a protective plate on his back. The soldier strapped the carrier onto his back and immediately departed with it. It was important for the soldiers carrying the frames to minimise the amount of time they were carrying them, so once the carriers were strapped on, each soldier went back up the main hall, through the gap in the wall, through the gaps in the fences, then across the bridge and down onto the beach. Once there, the carriers were immediately unstrapped and stacked in the boats.

In less than twenty minutes, the job was done. As soon as the last carrier had been loaded, the boats carrying them were launched, and began the trip back out to the submarine. Even if the rest of the assault force had to be abandoned, the most important thing was to secure the carrier frames and their contents.

As the operation was going on, Qasim spoke to Alan Southam. "If we are taking you as a hostage, then it will be best if you write a letter, which we will have permitted you to write, explaining that you have been taken hostage, if that's the line you wish to take."

Southam nodded. "Perhaps if we go up to the main office."

They walked up the main hall to the office.

"It would be best if you keep it brief," said Qasim. "In any case, we don't have much time."

As suggested, Southam kept the letter short, saying merely that he had been seized by unidentified armed men who had suddenly appeared in the main equipment bay, and had been told that he was being taken hostage. But at the end, he added:

"Tell Rachael I love her, and always will."

Qasim glanced at the letter and nodded. "Just leave it on the desk."

Outside in the main hall, Sergeant Hussain was waiting for them. "Everything's done, sir. The last group is ready to leave now."

"Are the British still securely locked in that room?"

"They are. We've also heard sounds that indicate that they've tried to barricade the door on the inside."

Qasim nodded. "Excellent." He looked down the main hall at the last four soldiers standing near the entrance to the main equipment bay, and raised his voice. "Right, that's it. Let's go!"

The soldiers walked up the main hall to join Qasim and the others. Lieutenant Qasim was the last to step through the gap in the wall out into the night, preceded by Alan Southam. As they were walking across towards the fence, a man suddenly appeared from behind building B1600 and began walking towards them. He walked forward a short distance, then stopped when he saw that something was going on.

What happened next took only a matter of seconds, but to Alan Southam, it seemed like a lot longer. He also stopped when he recognised the man as Hank Williamson. It was a strange fate that the man who in many ways epitomised everything he hated, and who, more than anyone, was responsible for triggering this whole train of events, should appear at this moment. Suddenly, it seemed as if all the perspectives in this complex affair were focused in that one place, in the 50 metres or so that separated the two men.

Hank Williamson saw the hole in the south wall of B1602; saw the soldiers emerging from it; and finally, saw Alan Southam, and recognised who it was. It was impossible for Williamson to know the journey that Southam had travelled since that fateful interview; but in that instant, intuition gave him understanding of what he was looking at. He knew all about Project Mayfly, and the possible implications of it; and with understanding, it was not hard to guess what was happening, and where the soldiers might have come from. And when he recognised Alan Southam, it was not hard to guess what he was doing there.

Hank Williamson had crushed this nonentity of a worm with his heel, assuming he would crawl away and die somewhere, which was what was expected of his sort. Instead, he had evidently had the temerity to try and bite back, to threaten Williamson's whole position with an act of betrayal. Williamson's reaction was rage: rage against the betrayal, but above all, rage against this affront to his authority.

Rage was the last emotion Hank Williamson felt, as Sergeant Abdullah squeezed the trigger of his assault rifle. Abdullah was as good as his word. The single shot hit Williamson in the chest, knocking him over backwards, and leaving him lying sprawled on his back on the concrete. The shot made little more than a muffled popping sound because of the silencer on Sergeant Abdullah's rifle, and was only just audible to Alan Southam and Lieutenant Qasim.

Southam stared in astonishment, not quite understanding what he had seen. Qasim, however, knew that Sergeant Abdullah was providing cover, and after quickly looking round, walked over to where Williamson was lying. But he needed no more than a glance to see that Williamson was dead. He hurried back.

"He's dead," he said to Southam. "We have cover." He pointed at the mound. "Hurry, we have no time to lose."

Southam did not need any further prompting. Although he hated Williamson, it was still a shock to see him shot, and it underlined the starkness of the situation. He walked forward and stepped through the gaps in the fences. Major Khan was waiting on the other side. He briefly shook Lieutenant Qasim by the hand and congratulated him on a successful operation. But there was no time for more than brief congratulations. Time was now short.

Most of the soldiers and all the equipment had now gone back across the bridge, with just Major Khan and Sergeant Abdullah remaining at the defensive post on the mound. Now they all crossed the bridge and went down onto the beach. By this time, most of the boats had gone. Only two remained for this last group. Alan Southam stepped into one of the boats with Sergeant Abdullah and two other soldiers. Lieutenant Qasim shoved off, then climbed in over the bows. Major Khan was the last off the beach, shoving the last boat off before climbing aboard himself. The boats were paddled out to about 100 metres from the shore before the engines were started.

Alan Southam had experienced a moment of emotion as he stepped into the boat. It would almost certainly be the last time he would stand on British soil. He had been thinking about his daughter Rachael since writing the letter on Qasim's instructions a few minutes earlier. Would he ever see her again? How would she think of him in years to come? Would she ever understand if she knew what had really happened? This was his moment of triumph, and yet in that moment, he felt sombre. Not even the sight of Hank Williamson left sprawled on the concrete had been enough to change his mood.

He watched the lights of Sellafield receding astern as the boats steadily bored out to sea. Under the cloudy sky, it was still almost completely dark, so that he could only just make out the others in the boat, and at that point, he was still not sure where they were headed. Only Lieutenant Qasim and Sergeant Abdullah, with their night-vision goggles, could see their objective: the long, low shape of the submarine, with the *Maid of Cork* keeping station just to the south of it.

As they approached the submarine, the boats turned north to swing round the submarine's bow and come alongside on its seaward side. As each boat came alongside, members of the submarine's crew were waiting for it with boathooks. They held it steady whilst those on board scrambled up onto the submarine's hull, then they hauled the boat itself up onto the hull. Opening quick-release valves deflated the boat in seconds. The engine was detached, the boat quickly folded up, and both were passed down through an open deck hatch into the hands of crew waiting below. Each boat was unloaded and stowed in less than ninety seconds.

As the soldiers scrambled down through the hatch one by one, Lieutenant Qasim indicated to Alan Southam that he should follow. Southam climbed down through the hatch and down the ladder, to find himself in a scene of organised confusion. His first impression was that everything was rather cramped. He was in a forward accommodation space which at that moment was very crowded. Soldiers were unstrapping equipment and weapons. These were being packed away in racks and stowage containers by members of the submarine's crew, with the soldiers helping once they were free. Most of the equipment, including the last of the boats to be brought back on board, was then being passed forward through an airlock door into the next compartment forward, with some of the soldiers following.

Qasim tapped Southam on the shoulder and indicated that he should follow. Qasim walked down to the forward end of the compartment, where there were a number of cubicles on either side of the gangway just in front of the airlock door. These were evidently accommodation for officers, even though they were very small – barely a metre wide, and less than two metres deep, against the curve of the submarine's inner hull. Each cubicle had a narrow bunk, an overhead rack and a small locker, and was accessed by a narrow door that opened inwards. Qasim opened the door of one of the cubicles.

"This will be your billet whilst you're on board. I'll be in the one next door."

Even as he spoke, an alarm sounded, and warning lights started flashing. A crewman scrambled up the ladder and swung the deck hatch down, and closed and locked it.

"We're diving," said Qasim.

As he climbed onto his bunk, Southam felt a slight unsteadiness, indicating that the submarine was now under way. With its hatches now closed, the submarine turned its bow west, then south-west. As it did so, the sea foamed around its hull as compressed air was released from the ballast tanks and the sea flooded in. In less than a minute, it had disappeared beneath the surface.

On the *Maid of Cork*, Ahmed pushed the engine throttle open. As the boat gathered way, he swung the wheel and steered south-west to keep station with the now hidden submarine.

14

The bad news travelled slowly at first. By 4.30 am it was fully daylight; but although a number of vehicles had passed along the access road by 7.30, no one noticed that anything was amiss. The two individuals in the vehicles who did notice Hank Williamson's body didn't realise what they were looking at, as it was too far from the road to be identifiable – they assumed it was a piece of debris. It was only at 7.30, when Bob Thompson, shift manager of the day shift, arrived at the B1600 complex, that things started to happen.

Thompson was the first of the day shift to arrive. He parked his car, walked over to the gate and let himself in with his swipe card. He had noticed something on the ground on the other side of the fence as he approached the gate. After going through the gate, he started to walk towards the entrance to B1602. As he did so, he began to realise that the object lying on the ground a little distance away to his left was not some piece of debris, but the body of a man. He stopped, then slowly walked over to where the man was lying. Even before he reached the body, it was obvious that the man was dead. There was a red-stained hole in the centre of his chest, which even Bob Thompson recognised as a bullet hole. The man's eyes were open in a fixed stare, and his jaw hung open. Thompson's sense of horror was compounded by shock when he realised that he recognised the man: it was Hank Williamson.

His only thought now was to raise the alarm. He hurried over to the entrance to B1602 and let himself in. Almost immediately, he realised that something was wrong. By this time, members of the night shift should have started assembling in the main hall in preparation for the handover between shifts. But there was no one about – the place looked deserted. He suddenly noticed light streaming in through a hole in the south wall to his left. How had that happened? However, his main concern was still to raise the alarm. He went down to the main office. He would normally have expected the night shift manager to be waiting for him to do the handover; but the office was empty.

He picked up the receiver of the desk phone, and tapped in the emergency number for the site police, before realising that the phone was dead. He put the receiver down and tried again, but it was still dead. He slammed the receiver down and went down to the next office. But the phone there was dead too. He went to the next office along – but all the phones were dead. He went back out into the main hall, but it was still deserted.

He called out: "Hello!" But there was no response. Something was seriously wrong. He walked down to the bottom end of the main hall and into the main equipment bay. It was like the *Marie Celeste*. Everywhere was deserted. The door to the radioactive store was open, but the store was empty. The reactor control room was also empty.

He went across to the rest room to see if there was anyone in there. He rattled the handle when he found he couldn't open the door. It was only when he looked down that he noticed the wire looped around the handle and running along the wall to the next door along. He walked along to unfasten it, but the other end had been secured with a metal crimp. He would need a wire cutter or something to cut through it. He went back to the rest room door. He rattled the handle and knocked on the door.

"Hello! Is there anyone in there?"

He heard muffled noises from the other side of the door. He called out again.

"Hello! Is there anyone in there?"

After a moment, a voice answered him from the other side of the door.

"Who's that? Who's speaking?"

"It's Bob Thompson. Is that Dave Turner? What the fuck are you doing in there?"

"Have the soldiers gone?"

"Soldiers? What soldiers? There's no one here. The place is deserted. There's a wire cable round the door handle. I'll have to find a wire cutter before I can open the door. The phones are all dead. I need to go across to the police post to raise the alarm. Can you hang on in there for a few more minutes?"

"Aye, we can hang on. But hurry!"

Bob Thompson ran back up the main hall and let himself out through the main entrance. Outside, he found Andy Barlow, who had also arrived early for the day shift. Andy was white-faced, having just seen Hank Williamson's body.

In answer to Andy's unspoken question, Bob Thompson said quickly: "There's been some kind of armed attack during the night. I'm going across to the police post to raise the alarm. All the phones in there are down. The night shift have all been locked in the main rest room. Can you go in and let them out? You'll need to get some wire cutters from out of the tool store. A wire cable's been tied round the door handle jamming the door shut. I've talked to Dave Turner through the door and told him I'm going to raise the alarm."

Andy Barlow nodded, then walked to the entrance to B1602 and let himself in. Bob Thompson ran back to the car park, jumped into his car, and tore down the 200 yards of road to the police post at the old Main Gate. He stopped outside the building in a squeal of tyres and brakes. An astonished Keith Wilson was in the process of going through the routine preparations for the shift handover at 8 am. His expectations of a quiet end to the shift were about to be rudely shattered.

Wilson immediately raised the alarm, and within a few minutes other police officers and senior managers began arriving at the B1600 complex. By the time Bob Thompson got back to B1600, there were already two police cars there, and other cars were arriving even as he was. A police officer was controlling access to the B1600 complex, and told Bob Thompson that the members of the day shift were to go to B1600 and wait there until they were given clearance to go into B1602, which had temporarily been sealed off. As he walked towards B1600, he saw members of the night shift emerging from the entrance to B1602 – Andy Barlow had managed to release them from the rest room. The night shift were being taken over to B1600 for an initial debriefing by the site police before being allowed home.

More police cars arrived, and there was a lot of activity in the area around where Hank Williamson's body still lay. Another car arrived, and the General Manager got out, and made his way, grim-faced, over to the gate.

It still took a while to establish the full extent of what had happened, but things started to move once the central fact had been confirmed: that all the irradiated sheets, as well as the replacement sheets of enriched uranium, together with their carrier frames, were missing. Once this had been confirmed, there was little doubt that the sheets had been the objective of the raiders.

This still left a lot of unanswered questions. Who were the raiders? Where had they come from? How had they got in? And above all, how had they evidently known so much about B1602, its layout, its routines, and what went on there?

It was only after all the night shift had gathered in B1600 that it was established that Alan Southam was missing. A search of B1602 confirmed that he was nowhere in the building. A search of the other buildings confirmed that he was nowhere in the B1600 complex; but his car was found in the car park by the entrance. There was a flurry of activity as other vehicles were moved away from it while the police attempted to open Southam's car. But when they finally succeeded, there was nothing of any interest inside.

Eventually, someone noticed the letter on the desk in the main office of B1602. It seemed to offer an explanation, and yet...

The 'gates' cut into the B1600 complex fence and the fence around the strip were fairly quickly discovered.

The grass covering the strip was well trodden with boot marks, which led fairly clearly to the conduit for the waste discharge pipes. They also led to the spot where a quantity of earth had recently been dug out from the west side of the mound. The trail led inevitably across the bridge, where the hole in the fence around the compound where the waste discharge pipes reached the ground on the spit was discovered. From there, the trail of boot marks led down onto the beach. It was clear that this was where the raiders had landed.

But where had they come from? And, perhaps more to the point, where had they gone?

15

Lieutenant Duncan McGill picked up his binoculars again and scrutinised the horizon ahead. He was standing on the upper bridge of HMS *Advance*, the Royal Navy patrol boat based in Liverpool. The upper bridge was open to the weather, and although it was late June, it felt chilly under a cool, overcast sky. The overcast also meant that visibility was not good. The atmosphere was misty, and visibility was down to about 20 miles. They would therefore be relying a lot on their radar.

It was 0630 hours, and they were half an hour out of Liverpool, heading north-west towards the Isle of Man. McGill had been asleep in his bunk when the alarm call had roused him just over an hour earlier. He had cursed when he was told the reason for the alarm. They were off on another wild goose chase after the elusive trawler that had periodically been intruding into British waters, apparently from a port in the Irish Republic.

It was the third time in as many weeks. It had made at least two incursions into Liverpool Bay, the last one almost to the mouth of the Mersey. *Advance* had been visiting Belfast at the time, and although they had sailed as soon as the news had come through, they had not been able to intervene. The previous week, it had intruded as far north as St Bees Head. At the time, *Advance* had been visiting Barrow in Furness, and again, they had given chase. On that occasion, they had almost caught it – it had just too much of a lead, and had managed to reach Irish waters with a few hundred metres to spare. McGill's remit did not allow him to cross into Irish waters, so, frustratingly, they had had to watch it escape.

However, they had got close enough for McGill to have a good look at it. The boat had not been carrying any identification marks, and was therefore anonymous, apart from a rather tatty Irish tricolour flying from the short mast on its cabin roof. Many trawlers, although not all, carried a two-letter code followed by a number, to indicate the vessel's home port; but this boat had no markings on it at all that he could see.

The three crew members that he could see didn't look Irish, somehow, or Northern European. Mediterranean? But such things meant little these days. They hadn't seemed in the least concerned that they were obviously being pursued – two of them had been lounging over the gunwale, idly watching as *Advance* closed the distance between the two vessels. They hadn't responded to radio messages, and if the boat had a transponder, it was switched off. On that occasion, the RAF had diverted a patrol plane that had happened to be airborne over the North Sea, to investigate the trawler; but although the plane had buzzed the vessel several times, it had not had any effect. It had confirmed McGill's view that if you wanted to effect a proper interception at sea, you needed a ship, not a plane.

McGill's irritation was increased by the fact that, this time, there was virtually no chance of their catching the elusive trawler. Its position had been given as just east of the Isle of Man, and they were setting out from Liverpool. Even at 25 knots, it would take them a couple of hours to reach the area of the Isle of Man, which would be more than enough time for the trawler to reach Irish waters. If the Navy wanted to rule the waves, it needed the ships to do so. It didn't always require multi-billion pound aircraft carriers to maintain an effective presence. A few more boats like *Advance* would cost a fraction of the amount wasted on duff computer projects by Whitehall every year, but would be money far more effectively spent. At a pinch, *Advance* could carry a fair bit more weaponry and equipment than she was listed for. It would be useful to have a boat based in the Isle of Man; but it didn't look as if that was likely any time soon.

McGill's sense of irritation gradually eased once they were at sea. It was a June morning, and although it was grey and overcast, the weather was calm, and the sense of freedom at being at sea lifted his spirits. Even if they didn't catch the bloody trawler, it would be another day at sea. The smell of fried bacon wafted up from the galley, where Able Seaman Steve Withington was cooking breakfast. There were five of them on board, constituting *Advance*'s basic operational crew: McGill was in command; CPO Harcourt was Executive Officer; CPO Howells was the Marine Engineering Officer; PO Watts was the Weapons Engineering Officer; and Steve Withington was the ship's Yeoman. On a routine voyage, they would also be carrying a number of university students from the University Royal

Naval Unit; but students were not carried on operational voyages. After the last two attempts to catch the trawler, they had had to go back to Belfast and Barrow to collect the students who had been left behind.

By 0700, it was clear that they were not going to catch the trawler. It was still misty, and visibility was poor; but having identified their quarry, they kept a watch on it on their radar, tracking it among several other trawlers in the area to the south and east of the Isle of Man. They were aiming for the point where their quarry would cross into Irish waters, assuming it continued on its present course, as the nearest point of interception. But it was clear that they were not going to catch the trawler. At 0736 they watched on the radar screen as it crossed the line into Irish waters. McGill decided that they would carry on to the point where it had crossed the line, so that he could at least say that he had done what he could under the circumstances.

At 0817, as they were approaching that location, the first message came through from HMS *Eaglet*, the shore station in Liverpool where *Advance* was based. The message merely told them to stand by for a high-priority signal. This came through five minutes later, just as they reached the point where McGill had planned to turn and set course for Liverpool. Charlie Harcourt received the message and took it off the printer after putting it through the decoder.

"Someone's got their knickers in a twist," he commented as he gave the signal to McGill.

The signal was headed "Top Secret", followed by "Priority: Immediate". It was addressed to McGill personally, as officer commanding HMS *Advance*. The signal authorised him to cross into Irish waters, including

Irish territorial waters if necessary, in pursuit of the trawler. He was to catch up with it, but only to keep station with it just out of small arms range, and await further instructions.

McGill made no attempt to conceal his surprise. "I wonder what the hell's going on?" he said. "Set a course to intercept, Charlie; but I'm going to need more information than this. I'll see what I can get out of them."

As Charlie Harcourt set *Advance* on her new course, McGill went down to the communications centre. After the preamble, using the same classification and priority, he sent:

"Have set course to intercept. Request instructions for if we are intercepted by a vessel of the Irish Navy."

He encoded it and sent it off. It was ten minutes before he received a reply, which contained only the terse message:

"Instructions to follow. Please wait."

However, he noticed that while the previous signal, although routed via HMS *Eaglet*, had originated from MOD Main Building, apparently from the office of the Secretary of State, this last message had originated from the Cabinet Office. The Cabinet Office was also the source of the next message. After an extensive preamble, it got to the point:

"A military attack has taken place upon the United Kingdom. Armed raiders have broken into the Sellafield site and seized a quantity of highly classified nuclear material which is potentially usable for the creation of nuclear weapons. It is essential that, if at all possible, this material is either recovered or destroyed. The raiders appear to have landed from the trawler you have been pursuing. The trawler was tracked to a location off Sellafield shortly before the raid took place, and was seen to leave shortly after the raid ended. Information about the raid has reached London only within the last hour. You are instructed to catch up with the trawler and maintain station with it, but just beyond small arms range. The raiders are heavily armed. Your task is to keep *Eaglet* notified of the trawler's position until other forces can be deployed to intercept and capture or destroy the vessel. The Irish Prime Minister has been advised of what has happened, and has given his consent to this course of action. You are likely to be contacted by a vessel of the Irish Navy, which may join you in keeping station with the trawler. You will be updated as the situation develops. Acknowledge immediate."

"It looks," said Charlie Harcourt philosophically, "as if there's been a cock up. And not just any old cock up either, but a whacking great bloody dong."

"Well," observed McGill in the same vein, "only politicians have dongs that big. I wonder who'll be clearing up the consequences?"

As *Advance* closed the distance to the trawler, their course swung from north-west to west. The trawler, having swung west after clearing the southern end of the Isle of Man, had now resumed a south-westerly course. Visibility was still poor, and even with binoculars, McGill still couldn't make the trawler out. Their radar screen showed that they were steadily closing on it, however. Eventually, when they were less than 18 miles distant, McGill finally caught sight of it through the binoculars, although it was still difficult to make out much detail. They continued to close on their quarry. When they were about 15 miles distant, the trawler crossed in front of a large freighter which was steaming due south, and then disappeared behind it. A couple of minutes later it reappeared as the freighter continued southwards.

As they closed on the trawler, McGill was studying it closely through binoculars. Five miles... 2 miles... 1 mile... 800 metres... still they closed. By this time, the feeling was growing on McGill that something was amiss.

At 500 metres, they slowed to keep station with the trawler at that distance. McGill sent a brief signal to HMS *Eaglet* to advise that they had now caught up with their quarry. McGill could now see every detail of the boat, and as he continued to search it through the binoculars, he could see no one on board. After another minute, he came to a decision.

"Charlie, I'm going to take the dinghy and board that boat. I've been looking at it for some while now, and I don't think there's anyone on board."

He handed the binoculars to Charlie Harcourt, who studied the boat for a minute, then nodded.

"I can't see anyone either."

"Keep station at five hundred metres, and stay ready to turn quickly in case it's a trap. Whatever happens, it'll happen quickly. It's either a trap, or something very odd's happened."

The dinghy was cleared for action and dropped into the water alongside. McGill strapped on a lifejacket and a steel helmet.

As he prepared to climb down into the dinghy, Steve Withington, who was standing by to release the dinghy, said, "You'll need someone to hold the dinghy alongside while you board, sir."

McGill stared for a moment. "I'm not asking you to come, Steve. If it is a trap, there'll be little chance of survival."

"I'm asking to come, sir."

McGill said nothing, but nodded and tapped Steve Withington lightly on the arm. Steve quickly donned lifejacket and helmet, and they both scrambled down into the dinghy. Steve started the engine and took the helm. The dinghy pulled away from *Advance* and skimmed across the water towards the trawler. PO Watts provided cover with a pintle-mounted 7.62 mm machine gun on *Advance*'s fo'c'sle.

As they approached the trawler, it seemed to McGill that it was lower in the water than it had appeared from the bridge of *Advance*. It also seemed to be slowing down. As they approached, there was still no sign of anyone on board. Steve Withington brought the dinghy alongside, and McGill managed to pass a line around a cleat on the trawler's gunwale, and pulled the two boats together. He scrambled up over the gunwale and onto the trawler's deck. As he did so, he noted that there was now no doubt that the trawler was low in the water.

The trawler was deserted. He went forward and into the wheelhouse, but there was no one there. He checked the wheel, confirming that it was locked. He went to the top of the companion-way down to the lower deck, but as he started to descend, he suddenly saw that he was confronted with an expanse of water. The lower deck was flooding: the boat was sinking. At that moment, the trawler's engine faltered, spluttered, and then stopped, as the water rose over it.

Steve Withington called out a warning from the dinghy. "Sir, I think she's going down!"

Even from the dinghy, with one hand grasping the trawler's gunwale, Steve could now look down onto the trawler's deck, it was so low in the water. McGill needed no further warning. The trawler was abandoned and sinking. It was baffling; mysterious. He could see no obvious explanation as he took a last, quick look round. But there was no time for more than that. He felt the trawler moving beneath his feet as it settled in the water. He climbed back into the dinghy and cast off.

Steve Withington opened the engine throttle and steered away from the doomed trawler, but circled round and came to a halt again about thirty metres away. They watched as the trawler sank. The sea poured over the gunwale, as first the hull, and then the wheelhouse disappeared beneath the surface. Last to go was the stubby mast, with the tatty Irish tricolour still attached. Then there were just huge bubbles of air and pieces of flotsam coming up from below, and spreading out on the surface amid a thin film of oil.

Steve Withington opened the throttle again, and the dinghy skimmed back to HMS *Advance*, which had come to a stop in the water as the trawler sank. Just as they reached it, an RAF Typhoon jet suddenly roared overhead at less than 500 feet. It turned, and circled *Advance* once, before climbing away again to the east, the noise of its engines fading into the distance as it did so. Then, they were alone on a calm sea.

16

As the Calf of Man passed astern to starboard, Ahmed swung the wheel of the *Maid of Cork* to bring them onto a new course, steering due west, and with the throttle, blipped the engine to signal the change of course to the submarine below them. He looked again at the radar screen, watching the progress of the blip which he knew must represent the Royal Navy patrol boat from Liverpool, and which was now obviously on a course to intercept them. Even as he watched, he saw it change to a more westerly course, clearly in response to their change of course. The radar indicated that it was moving at about 25 knots, or about two hours at that speed from their present position, and nearly three hours from the rendezvous point. As the *Maid of Cork* was about two hours from the rendezvous point, that left a reasonably comfortable safety margin.

It was not long after dawn, and in the early morning light, under an overcast sky, both the sky and the sea were a soft pearly grey colour. There was little wind, and the *Maid of Cork* was motoring steadily over an almost calm sea. The change of course was intended to shorten the time it would take to reach Irish waters, even though this would only be the Irish economic zone, rather than territorial waters proper.

Ahmed had no doubt that the British would cross into Irish waters in pursuit once news about the raid reached London, and its implications were understood; but it would take time to get the necessary political clearance for that, and that should give them enough time to reach the rendezvous point. The main uncertainty related to how quickly the raid would be discovered. If they were unlucky, and the raid was discovered quickly, there might not be much of a safety margin before they reached the rendezvous point, and the timing would be tight.

But the radar screen was now also showing their rendezvous contact. The MV *Buchanan*, a Liberian-registered freighter, was steaming south, parallel with the Irish coast, having left the port of Greenore in County Louth about an hour earlier. The *Buchanan* had arrived at Greenore a couple of days previously to deliver a bulk cargo of timber from Morocco. The shipping company that owned the *Buchanan* was itself owned by a series of shell companies, which in turn were controlled by a very discreet bank account in Monrovia. *Buchanan* was now in transit to Egypt, where it was due to pick up a cargo of raw cotton for export to Pakistan. However, on the way, it had an important but discreet function to perform.

At 0736, the *Maid of Cork* crossed the line into the Irish economic zone. Once they were in Irish waters, Ahmed swung the wheel to bring the boat back onto a south-westerly course for the run-in to the rendezvous point, blipping the engine again as he did so as a signal to the submarine.

As he watched the radar screen, he saw the Royal Navy patrol boat alter course slightly in response. It was still on a course to intercept them, and as Ahmed watched, it continued on that course. They must be able to tell that the *Maid of Cork* was now in Irish waters. Had news of the raid now reached them?

Up until now, the presence of the patrol boat, on this occasion as well as on previous occasions when they had played cat and mouse with the Royal Navy, was almost certainly because of their propeller. The plastic attachments to the propeller and the keel made their propeller very noisy when the boat was under way. This was for the benefit of the underwater listening devices which the intelligence people said that the British had placed in various locations in the Irish Sea, primarily to listen for submarines. The noise from the *Maid of Cork*'s propeller was intended to mask the noise from the submarine beneath them. But it also provoked a response from the British, who would be irritated by a trawler with a very noisy propeller cruising around the Irish Sea. Hence, the Royal Navy patrol boat.

Thus far, they had managed to avoid interception, despite some cheeky intrusions into British waters. Security considerations about the listening devices meant that the British would have to be cautious about the nature of their response. It was a job which would have to be done by the Navy. But after years of salami slicing of the defence budget, and years of mismanagement, and the over-concentration of the resources of all three services in southern England, the Navy was thinly stretched in places like the Irish Sea.

The clearest sign that the raid had been discovered would be the appearance of low-flying military aircraft; but although the Royal Navy patrol boat continued to advance towards them, so far there were no signs of military aircraft. It looked as if their luck was holding.

At length, Ahmed caught sight of the *Buchanan* to the west of them, through his binoculars. Even through binoculars, the ship was no more than an indistinct grey shape on the edge of vision at first. As the minutes passed, it became clearer, until he could even see it with the naked eye. He picked up the infra-red signal lamp which had been passed to him from one of the commando boats, and flashed a signal to the *Buchanan*. He repeated the signal. Mehmed, who was standing beside him, and now watching the ship through the binoculars, saw a member of the *Buchanan's* crew walk along the entire length of the ship's port rail, from the stern to the bow, and back again. It was the answer to their signal.

"They've spotted us," said Mehmed, as he continued to watch the ship.

Ahmed watched on their radar screen as the *Buchanan* slowed slightly, so that the rendezvous would happen in the correct sequence. He turned his attention back to the Royal Navy patrol boat. It had continued to advance towards them, and when he calculated its position, he saw that it had now crossed into Irish waters. It was the clearest sign yet that the raid must now have been discovered. Mehmed passed him the binoculars, and through them, he could now just make out the patrol boat on the edge of vision. Although it was still coming towards them at 25 knots, it would not intercept them before the rendezvous. They would have maybe half an hour to spare, which was a reasonably comfortable safety margin. However, if the raid was now known about, the sudden appearance of military aircraft might change all that.

He passed the binoculars back to Mehmed. "It's now crossed into Irish waters," he said, indicating the patrol boat, "so they now know about the raid. Keep an eye open for aircraft."

Mehmed nodded.

Ahmed called out a warning to Ali, who was below decks, and then went aft to prepare the inflatable dinghy for launch. After a minute, Ali came aft to help him.

"I've set the timer," Ali said. A hole had been cut into the bottom of the trawler's hull, and a scuttling valve set into it. The valve would be opened automatically by the timer, which would then scuttle the vessel. When the dinghy was ready, Ahmed went forward to the wheelhouse again. He watched as they converged with the *Buchanan*, now looming over them off their starboard bow. They were still steering south-west, while the *Buchanan* was steering due south. They would cross the *Buchanan*'s course about 200 metres in front of the ship's bow. *Buchanan* would cover that distance in about twenty seconds, so the timing would be critical. When they were still 500 metres from the ship, Ahmed blipped the trawler's engine four times as a signal to the submarine. Beneath the surface, the submarine began to turn to align itself with the *Buchanan*, which was now clearly audible in the submarine's hydrophones when the trawler's engine was throttled back.

On the *Maid of Cork*, Mehmed went aft to wait by the dinghy with Ali. In the wheelhouse, Ahmed checked the radar screen again, checked that the wheel and the throttle were both locked, then watched as they passed in front of *Buchanan*'s bow, now menacingly close. As soon as they were past and on *Buchanan*'s starboard side, he picked up the binoculars and looked astern, focusing on the Royal Navy patrol boat. It was now about 15 miles distant, and he could clearly see its bow wave. Seconds later, it was blocked from his view as *Buchanan*'s bow crossed his field of vision like a great grey shutter.

As soon as the patrol boat was out of sight, Ahmed stepped out of the wheelhouse and called to the others to launch the dinghy. The dinghy was dropped over the port side, still being attached by lines fore and aft to the *Maid of Cork*'s gunwale. Mehmed and Ali scrambled down into the dinghy. Mehmed started its engine, and kept the dinghy under control while it was alongside the trawler. Ahmed threw a number of items overboard, including the infrared signal lamp and the night-vision goggles. He closed the wheelhouse door, then went aft and scrambled down into the dinghy. He and Ali cast off fore and aft, and Mehmed steered the dinghy away from the trawler, and skimmed across the water towards the *Buchanan*.

Mehmed brought the dinghy alongside the *Buchanan* – no easy feat, as the dinghy bounced about in the ship's wake. Lines were thrown down from the deck of the ship, and Ahmed and Ali managed to catch them and secured them to the dinghy fore and aft. A rope ladder followed, and Mehmed and Ali scrambled up it to the ship's deck, while Ahmed did what he could to keep the dinghy under control. He then seized the rope ladder with one hand and put one foot on the bottom rung, while with his other hand he reached back and cut the engine. He then followed Mehmed and Ali up the rope ladder. Members of the *Buchanan*'s crew hauled the dinghy out of the water and up to the ship's rail. By this time, Ahmed was climbing over the rail onto the deck of the ship. Mehmed and Ali helped to pull the dinghy over the rail onto the deck.

As the rope ladder was retrieved, Ahmed, Ali and Mehmed were escorted by the *Buchanan*'s First Officer aft to the main superstructure. As they went, Ahmed looked out over the rail at the abandoned *Maid of Cork*, now well astern of them and diminishing into the distance as it ploughed its way steadily south-westwards. It had been a useful little ship.

The *Buchanan*'s Captain was an Egyptian, and when they had been ushered into the captain's day cabin, he looked at them critically for a few moments. "I received instructions from the owners to pick you three up at this location. I don't know what this is about, but I know enough to know not to ask too many questions. I don't know if you have anything to tell me."

"It's best if you don't know what this is all about," said Ahmed. "The story is that you picked us up after our trawler got into difficulties and we had to abandon it. That's the story you should give out to the crew. It's not quite true, perhaps, but near enough. The trawler hasn't actually sunk, but it will be sinking any time now. We've fixed it for that to happen. You should be alright anyway once you're fully in international waters. You're aware that we're going to be picked up?"

"After the second rendezvous? Yes. But I've not been supplied with any details."

"It's another trawler. Again, it's best if you don't know too much; but you will put us off in the dinghy once the trawler's been identified. I'll need access to your radar screen when we make the second rendezvous, to confirm the contact with the trawler."

The Captain nodded. "If you'll wait here in the meantime, I'll have some food sent up."

The *Buchanan* continued steaming south, just outside Irish territorial waters, but still within the Irish economic zone. As the ship approached Dublin Bay, the Captain appeared in the day cabin, and took Ahmed through to the bridge. A seaman who was with him took Mehmed and Ali down to the main deck to prepare the dinghy for launching. Ahmed received some curious glances from the members of the watch on the bridge; but as he was with the Captain, nothing was said. They went over to the radar screen. Ahmed studied the screen for a minute. A number of radar contacts were visible at that moment. Without speaking, the Captain tapped the screen with a finger, indicating one of the blips. He handed Ahmed a pair of binoculars. The vessel was already visible as a grey shape off their starboard bow, perhaps 5 miles distant. At that point, even the binoculars didn't reveal all that much detail of the other vessel. It was a bulk cargo carrier, generally similar in size to the *Buchanan*. The MV *Edina* had left Dublin docks about an hour and a half earlier. It had delivered a bulk cargo of aluminium oxide from Conakry, and was now outward bound to Cape Town with a cargo of gypsum. Like *Buchanan*, *Edina* was Liberian-registered: to a different shipping company, but one which was also controlled by a certain very discreet bank account in Monrovia. But not many people knew that.

Ahmed studied the radar screen again. At least two of the contacts visible were clearly freighters: one inbound to Dublin docks, and one which had just left the dock entrance. On the edge of the screen to the west was what was probably a passenger ferry on its way to Liverpool. Ahmed focused on two of the blips. Both were quite small vessels compared to the freighters. One was about 8 miles south-south-east of their present position, coming towards them on a converging course. Ahmed found it with the binoculars. It was a trawler – an ocean-going trawler, quite a bit bigger than the *Maid of Cork*. It was almost certainly their pick-up vessel; but they would have to wait until they were closer to be sure.

The other vessel had just left Dublin docks. It was moving very fast – maybe as much as 25 knots; and it appeared to be on a course to intercept the *Buchanan*. Ahmed estimated that it was just under 20 miles away, which meant that it would intercept them in about thirty-five to forty minutes, if it maintained that speed and course. He guessed that it was almost certainly a patrol vessel of the Irish Navy. He searched for it with the binoculars, and after a minute he found it. It was still indistinct at that point – little more than a bow wave. He pointed it out to the Captain.

"Looks like you'll be having company in about forty minutes. We'll be gone by then," he said.

The Captain looked at the vessel through the binoculars, but made no comment. Ahmed tapped the radar screen again, this time indicating the trawler. The Captain looked at the vessel through the binoculars before looking back at the radar screen, and studying the blips representing the three vessels that were about to play out the next stage in the drama. The immediate task was the main rendezvous with the *Edina*, which was now about a mile off their starboard bow. On their present course and speed, they would cross *Edina*'s course about 500 metres astern of it.

That would be too close, so the Captain ordered, "Engines ahead, slow."

The vibrations from the engines diminished as the engine room complied with the order, and the *Buchanan* began to slow down. Ahmed watched as the *Edina* crossed their bow, still about half a mile away.

As it did so, the captain ordered, "Engines ahead, full."

Minutes later, they crossed *Edina*'s wake, now about half a mile astern of it. The temporary reduction in engine noise was the signal to the submarine, which had been keeping station with *Buchanan* under the surface, to link up with the other ship that was now audible in its hydrophones. As the *Edina* crossed the *Buchanan*'s bows, the submarine began to turn to take up its new station.

Ahmed now turned his attention to the trawler. It was now about 3 miles distant, and it was now close enough for Ahmed to see through the binoculars that it was flying the signal flag for the letter L, which was the agreed identification mark. *Buchanan* was flying the signal flag for the letter B, to identify the ship to the trawler. Ahmed tapped the radar screen, indicating the blip representing the trawler, and gave the thumbs up sign.

The Captain nodded, then gave the order, "Engines ahead, slow."

As the *Buchanan* began to slow down, Ahmed took a last look at the radar screen. The patrol vessel was now about 14 miles away, and was very definitely on a course to intercept the *Buchanan*. It looked as if the Royal Navy patrol boat crew, having presumably witnessed the sinking of the *Maid of Cork*, had registered the possible significance of the trawler having passed close to the *Buchanan* before it sank. The information must have been passed on to the Irish, who were evidently intending to intercept. But they were always one step behind…

Ahmed turned to the Captain. "Thanks for your help," he said. "And good luck."

They shook hands. A seaman escorted Ahmed down to the main deck, where the dinghy was now ready for launch. Secured by lines fore and aft, it was dropped over the port side and lowered to the water. The rope ladder was dropped down again, and Ahmed scrambled down it into the dinghy. He started the engine and brought the dinghy under control while Mehmed and Ali climbed down to join him. The lines were cast off fore and aft, and Ahmed steered away from the side of the ship.

He kept pace with the *Buchanan*, taking station about 100 metres off its port side. They were thus hidden from the Irish patrol vessel. Ahmed maintained station as he watched the trawler approach. The trawler had turned, and was now approaching the *Buchanan* on its port side. After it had dropped the dinghy off, the *Buchanan* had resumed full speed, so when it passed the trawler, the trawler would be hidden from view from the Irish patrol vessel only for a very short time. Timing was therefore critical, and Ahmed watched the trawler carefully, judging his moment. The trawler was going to pass the *Buchanan* about 200 metres off its port side, and Ahmed began to turn the dinghy even before the bows of the two vessels had crossed.

He passed astern of the trawler, so close that the dinghy bounced in its wake, before turning sharply to bring the dinghy alongside the trawler's starboard side, still out of sight from the Irish patrol vessel. Lines were thrown from the deck of the trawler and secured to the dinghy, followed by a rope ladder. Minutes later, the three of them were standing on the deck of the trawler while the dinghy was being hauled up out of the water.

The trawler was Spanish-registered; but Ahmed, Ali and Mehmed were once again among their compatriots. As with the crews of the other vessels, however, they did not know who the three were, or anything about what they had been involved in. They had merely been following a limited set of instructions. But even if they had been able to, the three were far too weary to go into explanations at that point. They all desperately needed sleep. After a brief meeting with the trawler's skipper, a few minutes later they were asleep in a cabin below deck.

And so the conspiracy succeeded. The Irish Navy patrol vessel intercepted the *Buchanan*, and ordered it to change course and put into Dublin Bay. No attempt was made to board the *Buchanan* at sea, as it was assumed that the ship had heavily armed troops on board. Once in Dublin Bay, it was ordered to anchor in the bay, where it was then boarded by Irish Army commandos. They found nothing: no troops; no weapons or military equipment; and no trace of the irradiated sheets or their carrier frames. British technicians, who followed the commandos on board once the ship had been secured, went over every inch of the vessel from stem to stern with Geiger counters; but there was no evidence that the sheets and carrier frames had ever been on board the *Buchanan*.

There was nothing else wrong with the *Buchanan* either. The ship's papers were all in order, and both the crew and the state of the ship complied with international and Irish maritime law. Everything was perfectly legal. Eventually, after protests from the *Buchanan*'s Captain, and then the shipping company, and finally the Liberian Government, the Irish authorities had to release the ship and allow it to resume its voyage.

HMS *Advance* had marked the location of the *Maid of Cork* with a buoy, and the following day Irish Navy scuba divers located the sunken vessel. It lay upright on the sea bed in about 140 feet of water. Although conditions were less than ideal, the divers were able to get inside the trawler and do a preliminary search of it. They did not find the irradiated sheets or their carriers, or any weapons, or anything else suspicious. Eventually, a salvage ship was brought to the scene, and the trawler was raised from the seabed and taken to Greenore, where it was left on the quayside. But despite the most detailed scrutiny by both Irish and British officials, nothing was found. The only unusual details were the attachments to the propeller and keel, and the scuttling valve.

When the *Buchanan* was finally cleared and released, the report from the Irish Navy patrol vessel that the ship had made a close pass with another trawler not long before it was intercepted then became significant. The trawler was eventually identified by information from the Irish Fisheries Protection Service. By this time, it had entered Spanish waters, so a request was sent to the Spanish authorities. But when the trawler was boarded by Spanish customs officials when it docked at its home port, again, nothing suspicious was found. It was not noticed that the trawler had somehow acquired three extra crew members since it left port. The three had been provided with forged but very legitimate-looking passports and identity documents, and everything seemed in order.

A great distance away, the submarine finally surfaced. It was out of sight of land, and no other vessels were in sight at that moment. Shortly after it surfaced, a helicopter appeared and made for the submarine. It was a civilian helicopter on a legitimate, registered charter flight. But it had a couple of unscheduled detours to make en route. The first took it to the submarine. It hovered just above the submarine's deck while the irradiated sheets in their carrier frames were passed up into the helicopter's open door.

Finally, a man climbed up into the helicopter from the submarine, and took his place in one of the rear seats. It was Alan Southam. With the door closed again, the helicopter lifted away from the submarine, which continued on its way, its mission now accomplished.

Once it was back over land, the second detour took the helicopter over a certain international boundary. It landed in a remote place less than a kilometre inside the country's border. A couple of cars and a van were at the spot waiting for it. Musa Khalid greeted Alan Southam as he stepped down from the helicopter, while technicians who were with him transferred the sheets in their carrier frames into the waiting van. The helicopter then lifted off and continued on to its legitimate destination.

Thus, the true identity of the raiders was never established. Even Miriam's information, when it eventually began to filter through from her hospital bed, could not help with that. She only had information about the act, not about the ultimate perpetrators.

It was only when information about the unusual attachments to the *Maid of Cork*'s propeller and keel reached the intelligence people in London, all other lines of investigation having drawn a blank, that it was realised that a submarine must have been involved in the fateful raid. But by then it was too late.

Carl Richardson
22 May 2016